The

A Parody

Standing rigging of a square-rigged ship, with reefers aloft unbending the sails.

Illustration source: Sirius Liber Marinaricus.

Courtesy of The Science and Technology Stunting Center
The Dr. Joey Institute Library, and The La Jolla Clam Foundation

1. Fore royal stay
2. Fore t'gallant stay
3. Fore top stay
4. Outer jibstay
5. Jibstay
6. Forestay
7. Jib boom
8. Bowsprit with figurehead
9. Bobstay
10. Dolphin striker
11. Hawspipe
12. Fore pigstick
13. Fore truck
14. Fore royal mast
15. Fore royal yard
16. Fore t'gallant mast
17. Fore t'gallant yard
18. Fore topmast
19. Fore topyard
20. Foremast
21. Starboard fore ratlines
22. Larboard fore ratlines
23. Starboard fore shroud
24. Larboard fore shroud
25. Royal backstay
26. Fore t'gallant backstay
27. Foretop backstay
28. Fore backstay
29. Fore royal larboard brace
30. Fore royal starboard brace
31. Main pigstick
32. Main truck
33. Royal stay
34. Main royal mast
35. Main royal yard
36. Main t'gallant stay
37. Main t'gallant mast
38. Main t'gallant yard
39. Main topstay
40. Main topmast
41. Main topyard
42. Main mast
43. Main yard
44. Main forestay
45. Superfluous stay
46. Starboard main ratlines
47. Larboard main ratlines
48. Main royal backstay
49. Main royal larboard brace
50. Main royal starboard brace
51. Main royal backstay
52. Main t'gallant backstay
53. Top main ratlines
54. Top main backstay
55. Master clothesline
56. Mizzen pigstick
57. Mizzen truck
58. Mizzen t'gallant stay
59. Mizzen t'gallant starboard shroud
60. Mizzen t'gallant mast
61. Mizzen t'gallant backstay
62. Spanker gaff topping lift
63. Mizzentop forestay
64. Mizzentop starboard shroud
65. Mizzen topmast
66. Mizzentop backstay
67. Spanker boom halyard
68. Spanker gaff
69. Spanker boom topping lift
70. Larboard spanker gaff vane
71. Starboard spanker gaff vane
72. Mizzen stay
73. Starboard mizzen ratlines
74. Larboard mizzen ratlines
75. Starboard timenoguy
76. Larboard timenoguy
77. Spanker boom
78. Spanker block
79. Pleonastic brace
80. Superogatory mizzen line
81. Fanny spanker
82. Nascent catharpings
83. Cringle stop
84. Stern fangle

O. BRIAN PATRICK

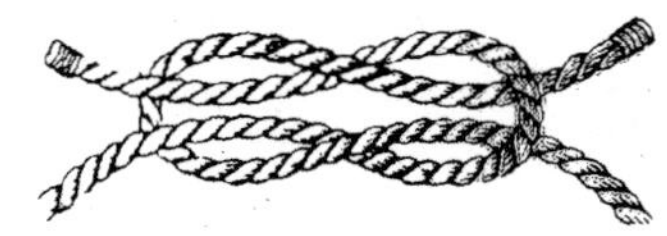

The Obversant Voyage

A Parody

INTERMITTENT PUBLICATIONS

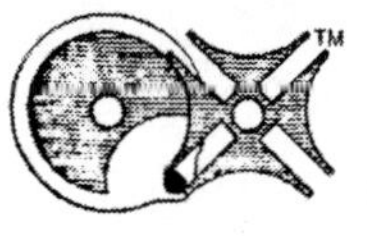

LA JOLLA

FOR R.A., WHO SPARED ME FROM A RABID PRESS-GANG AND THE TORTURES OF THE DAMNED

United States Library of Congress Control Number:
2005937241

ISBN: 0-9774915-0-1

INTERMITTENT PUBLICATIONS

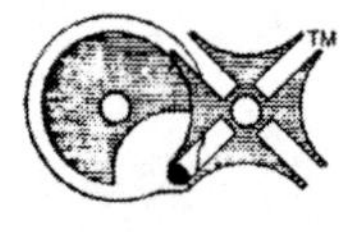

LA JOLLA, CA

Printed by hand in the United States of America

AUTHOR'S NOTE

Perhaps most authors are wholly original as far as their sentences or whole pages are concerned; indeed Shakespeare seems to have invented almost everything, while Chaucer borrowed money from both the living and the dead. And to come down to a somewhat parallel plane to the current one, the present writer is even more derivative than the supposedly derivative work this work is derived from, since for this book he has kept most doggedly to expropriating the terms, phrases, characters and situations, and even whole paragraphs, from another, similarly named author. But general appropriation in this case is virtually the same thing as downright plagiary, and in passing it must be confessed that beginning on Page One almost every word is a direct lift, since the present writer is in no way the trenchant rhetorician the distinguished author in question was.

If this kind of writing were to continue, however, it is clear that the writer would soon have a litigation thrust upon him by barristers for the legitimate publishers of the late author's fully legitimate books. Some five or six years ago, with the passing of that legitimate author, it was suggested that any additional book about the Royal Navy of Nelson's time would now have to be written by someone else. But if the publisher in question knew how much pleasure the present writer has taken--along with the blocks of text--in this kind of writing, or cribbing, if you must, it's hoped the legitimate publisher in question would be grateful not to receive any more similar submissions for legitimate consideration, and leave it at that. In the present book, the naval fictional historian will detect that this story takes place chronologically in the dead center of the Aubrey-Maturin oeuvre between *The Far Side of the World*, and *The Reverse of the Medal*, and though hitherto untold, it is nonetheless a true factual account of the fictional events that occurred between those two books. In course, it will become evident to the reader why this story was never--could never--be told, until now.

Yet the writer, while taking great liberties with copyright law, will adhere strictly to the style of the similarly named author with respect to fictional historical accuracy, and he will speak of the Royal Navy as it was spoken of in the author's books, making use of whole passages as boilerplates if necessary. For example: the reader will meet no cockatrices with looks to kill, no nymphomaniacal hottentots with enlarged breasts but without language or discriminating mating habits, no Chinese, perfectly scrutable, and skilled in any sciences beyond fireworks or railroad and canal building, no Englishmen attempting to pass themselves off as dancing bears, no wholly virtuous, ever-victorious, or even victorious *ever* characters. Further, although some of the heroes, due to continuity, may seem necessarily immortal, the writer cautions that they are not; and should any crocodiles appear, he undertakes that they may devour their prey without tears, but he cannot promise they will not require a gallimaufrous clyster to complete the task of digestion.

Chapter One

'Avast fighting!' Bellowed Captain Aubrey, ''Vast there, I say!' He looked directly at Joe Plaice who had just cruelly piked one of the Americans, a wonderfully horrible, livid wound that left part of an ear dangling. In Jack Aubrey's right arm, which was bloodied to the elbow, was a cutlass. With his left he withdrew a pistol from his breeches and fired a shot into the air. In the yawning stillness that followed both sides stood momentarily transfixed, and the yellow-haired captain turned to his coxswain: 'Bonden, get the name or identity of any man, *Surprise* or *Norfolk*, who so much as swings another boarding pike or picks up a belaying pin, and--' looking around at the crowd, 'He'll hang from the yardarm before we've doubled the horn to Barbados.'

'And which is where we intend to hang the *rest* of your lot...' hissed George Abel, very quietly, to a fellow whose face was still inches from his own. The American pulled back the corner of his mouth and spit back in a croaky whisper: 'Oh, I don't reckon it's yanks they'd be ahangin', cully.'

'You yankee jackeen...' started Abel, and then stopped, inhaled loudly through his nostrils, and stood, slowly seething, to his full height, never lifting his eyes from the other man's glower.

Most every other pair of eyes on the beach had been gaping across the lagoon in despair or exultation at the concluding drama just beyond the reef, and they were now focused on Jack as he sheathed his sword and put the pistol back in his breeches, grateful he'd remembered to borrow it from young Mr. Blackeney. Jack was a large man, fourteen or fifteen stone at least, but to the crew members of the *Norfolk* who had just witnessed his fighting persona for the first time he seemed in battle half again as large.

'Mr. Honey,' the acting third lieutenant snapped upright, 'Mr. Honey, take Mr. Nagel and Mr. Hollar and round up the prisoners. Mr. Lamb...Mr. Lamb?'

The carpenter was standing amidst the rack and ruin of his work, looking to and fro with apoplectic exasperation. 'Oh, Sir, look how them rogues done the cutter! They--' he suddenly composed himself, 'Yessir?'

'We shant be needing the cutter refit now, correct? But my best compliments, Mr. Lamb!' Jack's face softened a shade closer to his normal amiable countenance, and then, officious again: 'Mr. Lamb, see what you can contrive to secure those prisoners...those prisoners who may be uncooperative.' He turned to his clerk and said: 'Mr. Ward, get the names of each as they are assembled.' And he added privately: 'And a thoroughgoing description, pray; we're going to sort the true *Norfolks* from the *Hermiones*.' He looked around: 'Where's that Haines?'

'They... they scragged him, Sir.' said George Abel, who had helplessly witnessed the disembowelling moments after the whaler had appeared outside the lagoon.

Mr. Lamb's expression sadly darkened again, for the young cooper had been working alongside him, fashioning casks and assisting in the lengthening of the cutter by eight feet, when it seemed their only escape from this poorly charted island.

Jack's blue eyes narrowed slightly, 'Mr. Abel,' he said quietly, 'When the prisoners are assembled, see if you can pick out the blackgaurds that did the deed?'

'Aye Sir.' said Abel, 'Even if he were a peach, beggin' your pardon, Sir, and God rest 'is soul, Sir.'

Jack made no reply, but strode over toward the beach with his eyes clapped on *Surprise*, the joyous *Surprise*, as she let go her stunsails alow and aloft, struck her main, maintop, t'gallants and royals, slowly backed her fore topsail, and hove to about half a cable's length windward of her vanquished chase, the whaler *Wm. Enderby*.

Surprise was still cheering like a ship clean out of her mind with delight, whilst on board the whaler men with resolute faces scrambled amongst the fallen rigging of her main and fore t'gallant masts, and presently the mizzen backstay gave a twanging groan and the mizzen mast sprung at the cap. A seven inch larboard mizzen shroud snapped with a muffled crack and the force threw two men in the ratlines down hard into the clutter and chaos on deck.

A few hands were now peering forlornly over her bowsprit. There, a biscuit toss to larboard lay the sunken hulk of *U.S.S. Norfolk*, a commisserant victim of the same impertinent shoal. In their own way they were quite sunk, too, because of course *Enderby* was originally out of London, His Majesties ship once, and now again. The Americans had captured her and subsequently over laden her with the blubbery spoils of three other prizes, all of which they had burned to the waterline.

When she'd appeared hull up off the small cape the Americans dropped the last pretense of their *rue de guerre*--that peace had been declared--and vigorously attacked the greatly outnumbered *Surprises*. A red-headed midshipman and one of the youngsters from *Norfork* had frantically dashed out across the reef, gesticulating like telegraph pinafores, trying to warn the whaler off. *Norforks* had crowded the beach by the score, cheering and roaring, relishing this triumphant delivery. But with *Enderby* a mile or more off it was already clear she'd mysteriously spread far too much canvas for this insidious shore, and when *Surprise* loomed into view at her stern in prompt and brutal explanation, booming an admonishing rippling broadside to leeward, Fate's Weird Sisters took their last round turn for the day, victors and vanquished exchanged their status, and just as palpably they reciprocated their spirits.

High, high above, on the cliff, Stephen Maturin knelt peering over the edge where he and the Reverend Martin had viewed with fluctuant emotion the motions of the various *dramaticus personnae* far below. Stephen and his companion, both of a bent toward natural philosophy and not skilled hands as regards the cutter refit, had come up here ostensibly to forage for yams, of which they had in fact gathered many. But their main pursuit, their shared passion this afternoon, had been their annoyance of the flightless rail they had spotted scurrying along the edge of the brush on the side of the wash. Stephen turned to his companion and repeated: 'She's the joyful *Surprise*, Martin, God and Mary and Patrick be with her!'

Martin squinted down at the sea, blinking with his one good eye, and saw a launch and the jolly boat were already being let down from a pair of davits rigged near *Surprises*' stern. 'It appears our darkest hour came just before the dawn, Doctor.' Martin was a man as prone to cliché in casual speech as he was to plagiary in his formal sermons on shipboard. But on occasion, through his great effort, Martin was able to select just the right Donne, the fitting South, the apropos Barrow, to perfectly fadge the occasion. Stephen was reflecting that there are to be sure instances as well, such as the present one, where indeed one of Martin's clutch of shopworn platitudes answered like a haberdasher's waistcoat. Mere moments before there had surely seemed no rational cause for hope at all, at all.

Now, suddenly, the timeous arrival of *Surprise*, thundering in like a great white horse, brought their certain manumission. It came as a greater relief to Stephen, since he had felt somewhat responsible for the predicament he'd, however inadvertently, placed himself, Jack, and the rest in.

Had he not carelessly run in pursuit of a glimpsed bird, a great, prodigious bird; had he not tripped on the sole of the *Surprises'* gangway, falling into the waist of the ship; had he not struck his head on a gun breech and sunk into a shallow coma shortly before they fetched this meager island; had he not been taken ashore, more dead than alive, where Mr. Butcher, the surgeon of *Norfolk* had planned to perform a trepan procedure on Stephen's brain; had not a fierce, sky-rending squall torn *Surprise* from her mooring and blown her... who knew where for all love?; and finally had not Jack Aubrey--no doubt with best intent, Stephen thought, smiling briefly--had not

Jack and the others accompanied Stephen's gurney ashore where the operation was to be performed on *terra firma*...

Of course Stephen only knew most of this because he had been informed of it after his sensible recovery. For his part, Stephen could not now call to mind the suspected albatross, nor any events subsequent to its' sighting nor precedent to his eventual recovery before surgery had even begun.

It was perhaps just as well he was not aware of the undisguised delight with which Mr. Butcher had calculated upon utilizing Stephen's fine French patent trephine, and it doubtless spared him countless years of specious, unavailing study of the tobacco plant, that no one had noticed a pinch of Mr. Butcher's snuff absently fell under Stephen's nostril, causing him to sneeze coincident with his coming to himself.

Stephen cut short his meditations however, for this was not a case of: 'All's well that ends well,' as Mr. Martin could have reported had he not a more apt saw at his disposal that day. There were no doubt casualties below, and he and Martin began descending the scree to the beach as fast as ever they could.

In the event, few *Surprises* proved seriously injured. But including the unfortunate Haines there were three *Norfolks* dead and two more so gravely hurt that Stephen knew instantly that only Extreme Unction could serve them. He said a private rosary until first the one, and within thirty minutes, the other was taken up, and Stephen had closed the man's eyes and whispered: '...*Nunc et in hora mortis nostrae*..'

Stephen got up, walked across the runnel that until today's battle had served as *ad hoc* Tom Tiddler's Ground between the two camps, and joined Mr. Butcher, who was beginning to stitch up the remains of the American's ear. He had already removed the left eye of one of the whalers, who'd had the misfortune of being struck directly in the orb by a careening futtock stave when *Enderby's* mizzen shroud parted.

Stephen walked to where the man was sitting on a makeshift bench and observed his appearance. He was a smallish man, though strongly built, common traits in many sailormen he had tended. His remaining eye, which was green and shone like a Wedgewood teacup, betrayed an inner intelligence. He looked to Stephen like a man with bottom. With his left hand he was holding a bandage to his missing eye and with his right he clutched tight to a dark amber bottle of rum.

Looking at the man now, Stephen candidly scrupled the wisdom of such hasty excising of the organ. Barring infection, and with painstaking suturing (of just the kind Martin does so well in his avicular taxidermy) it was perhaps likely sight would have returned. Stephen pursed his lips. In large protracted ship-to-ship engagements he'd never time for this kind of reexamination and recrimination. The smoke and the screams, and the deafening roar of great guns banging away, the hopeless confusion, the scuppers running deep with blood, the decks perilously slippery with it, and the hurried *triage* in a cockpit splattered lurid red with it; all left no time for such reflection, let alone guilty reevaluation--leave that to the admiralty.

Well, after all, thought Stephen, isn't it Martin himself who does fine with *his* one eye? But still, he thought, to perhaps have merely impatiently extracted a possibly curable thing so very precious as an eye; 'That would be most "impatient"' he said quietly to himself. Perhaps he was feeling partially culpable. Not about the dead, of course; the dear knows a thaumaturgist couldn't have answered in either case. Nonetheless, Stephen's mind began to skirt the edge of a long precipice of doubt and stupid fear. How many countless controvertible corrigendum may he himself have committed in the past? Despite doing one's best, couldn't an omniscient observer point to errors, false presumptions, bad judgements or misplaced priorities, for every blessed contumacious situation in the life of a holy saint, for all love? No, a saint is a saint because he is not found wanting for the righteous, reverent thoughts and deeds of a saint. He is not overcome by absent-minded indolence.

Stephen's thoughts were interrupted: 'Doctor, I see you are appreciative of my work. A very tidy ablation, is it not?' Butcher gently removed the bandage and momentarily revealed the bloodied socket with undisguised pride.

Stephen looked to Butcher and then to the cyclops, considering what possible civil response to compose, when Jack walked up, aglow still with great relief of the day, to invite Stephen and Mr. Butcher to a special dinner the following evening in the gunroom aboard *Surprise*.

'I understand Killick began preparations late yesterday when they guessed the stern chase might put them in close proximity to our little island here. I so look forward to a right proper decent meal, don't you, Mr. Butcher?

'It is most kind of you, Captain,' said Butcher, and then, looking at Jack's bloodied arm, 'My goodness, Captain, you haven't savaged the right limb now as well, have you? No...no I see it's the spilt blood of others. The other has healed up rather well has it?'

Stephen remembered Jack's battered arm when they were prisoners aboard *U.S.S. Constitution*. The arm might just as likely have been lost, and yet Butcher had made a splendid task of mending it. Perhaps he should confine second guessing to his own medical practices.

'Yes...yes. It has healed quite capital, thankee, Mr. Butcher, and now that our situations are somewhat reversed I hope to extend the same measure of kindness as we received from yourself and your cousin Captain Lawrence.

'Of course,' Jack continued, 'Captain Palmer is doubtless not well enough to attend just yet, but--'

Heretofore Jack had not noticed the stolid mariner for whom Stephen was now fashioning an eye patch from a scrap of sailcloth.

'Whatever on earth struck your glassy out, my poor fellow?'

'I believe it were a spar or a small block, Sir. But it's quite proper seen to; and I see just as good with t'other, though I do still suffer a most profound headache, like.'

'Your English?' inquired Jack, 'Off *Enderby*?'

'Welsh, actually, if you please, Captain Aubrey, sir. My name's Jones; Tanzi Llangarcth-Jones, formerly mizzento' man for dear old *Enderby*, sir, at your service, if you please.'

'Well,' said Jack, 'You're a fine stoic and noble example of a Welshman, I'm sure. Pray, should you wish to--that is if you feel up to it--we should be honoured to have you join us tomorrow for supper in the gunroom of *Surprise*.'

‘’Tis I who would be most honoured, Captain, and most grateful for your sharing comestibles with an old salt, half daft and now half blind as well, so it seems.’

‘Excellent!’ said Jack, ‘And should you like to bring one of the squeakers from *Enderby* to be your server, please feel free, Mr. Jones.’

‘Oh, they just calls me Tanzi, Captain Aubrey, and I know just the nipper for the job. God bless you, Sir, we wouldn’t miss it for all the world!’

All the rest of that day and on through the second dog watch that evening every available boat had been engaged to busily criss-cross the little lagoon, to-and-fro, forth-and-back, ship-to-ship and ship-to-shore, moving men and supplies. The prisoners were all got aboard *Enderby*, though not without some strained moments. Acting Gunner Wilkens armed several of the original *Enderbys* to watch over their former captors, and Jack ordered a few *Surprises* and a brace of marines sent along as well.

Jack did not want the situation to become uglier, but without some care it most surely would. Those *Surprises* who’d been aboard all this time under Mowett’s command, and who’d subsequently returned draped in glory, they were beside themselves with smug joy. But those who had been marooned with Jack had been sorely disobliged by conditions, both natural and political, since their arrival. Jack knew he had made matters worse himself by driving the men hard the last three days. They had been driven very hard, and for most it was the only time they had ever seen Captain Aubrey employ a rope’s end.

Then three days ago, from high on the bluff, Jack had seen the white puff of sails, no doubt American sails, hull down, far, far to the northwest, and had sadly resolved that an expedient completion of the cutter refit was then the only recourse.

But even without the approaching ship, survival on the island was becoming more tenuous by the hour. Local flora and fauna, scant as it was, had been disappearing fast. The breadfruit and coconuts were long gone, and the ‘torch thistles’ gave every man who ate them the wet gripes. The native yams, barely amenable to human consumption at their best, were now scarcer than hen’s teeth.

Angling for the sharks thronging around *Norfolk's* hull proved almost more dangerous than their meagre flesh justified, and eating an innocent-looking codfish found along the reef induced a crimson eruption of the men's skin, accompanied by black vomit and then temporary loss of sight.

The four times more numerous Americans on the other side of the stream had been, if anything, worse off. Captain Palmer had become quite ill, and as his strength ebbed so his command, along with his people's discipline, seemed to wane proportional. His last communique to Jack had been via verbal messenger, since they'd had no paper, and certainly almost none of them had shoes except Mr. Butcher. The island's terrain varied between razor sharp coral rock, beaches strewn with volcanic glass, and a ground cover of spiny ivy wherever the dense undergrowth wasn't absolutely impenetrable. Nearly every man-jack was lame to one extent or another.

'Uncle Palmer's Paradise, indeed.' Jack said silently to himself. That's how Palmer's nephew, Captain Gill of *Acapulco* had described Old Sodbury's Island in a letter Jack had found amongst *Acapulcos'* papers when *Surprise* captured her off Chilé some weeks ago. It had helped lead him to this place, and they had indeed found Palmer and *Norfolk*, shipwrecked. It had, however, proved something less than paradisiacal, for all concerned.

Jack gazed at the island through the gracefully curving glass of the French-built *Surprises'* stern windows. Jack was not a man given to resentment, and even if he were he would not now resent Palmer's cheeky 'Give you joy of the peace!' greeting. Jack found it an amusing chimera, and he had smoked it right off anyway. Unfortunately, before long most everyone else did as well, and that, combined with Palmer's diminished grip on his crew, had been a growing concern to Jack as tensions grew between the two camps. On Thursday a man's arm was broken by a maul when some *Norfolks* tried to steal a compass saw from Mr. Lamb, and such skirmishes would surely have grown more frequent, and more consequential.

If all that weren't trouble enough for Paradise, there were the bleeding *Hermiones*. The damnable *Hermiones*. The doomed *Hermiones*.

There was a knock on the door accompanied by a metallic

rattle from the scabbard of Oakes, the marine sentry.

'If you please, Sir, Doctor Maturin to see you.'

'By all means...' said Jack, and Stephen could hear a rare weariness in his friend's voice even before he entered the captain's cabin.

'You look a bit hipped, my dear, what is it?' asked Stephen.

'Well,' said Jack, perhaps I am just a bit fagged-out. I'm very happy to be back aboard *Surprise*, of course, but this *Hermiones* situation is like a fly in my pudding.'

'How so, Jack? You refer to "Hermesian" do you not, Jack? The infamous theologian, Father George Hermes of Bonn? ....No?'

'No. *Hermiones*.' Jack was incredulous. 'Oh, really, Stephen, surely you're familiar with the sordid episode?' Jack tilted his head to one side and smiled affectionately at his friend in truly perplexed wonder, but Stephen's guileless expression as he blinked his pale blue eyes back at him was unmistakable.

'How could it be possible that sailing with me in a King's ship, when I could keep one under me, since the year one, you're unaware of the mutinous *Hermiones*? Perhaps they're not as famous as your *Bountys*, but they were more ruthless by half, I assure you.'

'I must confess ignorance, Jack,' said Stephen, 'although I do know something of poor Nelson...'

'Poor Nelson?' said Jack, non-plussed.

'Yes,' said Stephen, 'He was once an acquaintance--'

'An acquaintance?' blurted Jack, 'Lord Nelson?' and immediately wished he hadn't, as it occurred to Jack that perhaps Stephen was still a bit deranged from his bang on the head, after all.

'No, no, Jack, not *Lord* Nelson, for all love, *David* Nelson, the botanist Lord Banks sent aboard *Bounty* to tend the breadfruit saplings.'

'Oh, David, of course, no relation...' said Jack, greatly relieved. 'Poor chap. Survived with Bligh in that open boat for over a thousand leagues of shifting tropic seas, hostile islanders, and rations that make our recent castramentation look like a bloody royal garden party....only to cop it in Batavia, as I recall. No doubt, Batavia; the most fusty, fetid, fuggy, frowzy, *frowsty* backhouse port on earth. I dare say it's enough to kill anyone.'

Jack looked thoughtful: 'You know, one of the men with Bligh, only one, Quartermaster John Norton, didn't complete the voyage. If I recall he was killed by Indians when he tried to haul anchor in one of the Friendly Islands, and that was the last time Bligh weighed 'til they fetched East Timor.'

Both men sat in silence for a moment and presently Jack said: 'Bligh might be the best navigator in the Royal Navy, and why not with Cook for a schoolmaster? But he has always been very taut; too taut by at least half, and even now I understand he's had more discipline problems at his post in New Holland, poor fellow.

'Of course, Jack continued, the real scrub blackgaurd in the *Bounty* fiasco has turned out to be Edwards.'

'Edwards?' asked Stephen.

'Yes. The one they sent in *Pandora* to Otaheite to find the mutineers,' replied Jack.

'Well, yes, I do seem to recall,' Stephen ran his fingers lightly across his forehead, 'Caged, they were, chained naked on deck, or some such barbarous naval notion of justice. What's that they called it?'

'*Pandora's* box,' said Jack. 'Most of them had turned themselves in to Edwards, since they were never among the active mutineers. But Edwards gave them almost no food or water, and no head privileges whatsoever. In the tropics; imagine!'

'Thank you, Jack, but I'd rather not just now, if it's all the same to you.'

'When he ran the cursed *Pandora* up on a reef he ordered his first to *stop* unshackling the prisoners as she sank fast. Those that drown in *Pandora's* box turned out the lucky ones. The rest survived only to be more cruelly used by this Edward Edwards, a disgrace to his rank and country, though I've not a very strong opinion on the blackgaurd compared with some, Stephen!' laughed Jack.

'And you may not know *Hermiones*,' said Jack, but they certainly know *Surprise*. *Hermione* was a thirty-two gun fifth-rate frigate. Oh, she was a sweet sailor, built at the Bristol yard, 1780's. In '97 she was off the West Indies when her crew mutinied against her Captain, Hugh Pigot, another blackgaurd that should never have been made post. He'd made the *Hermione* a hell afloat alright, but unfortunately they didn't stop at relieving him of command, they killed him, along with three lieutenants, the marine officer, the purser, the bosun, the clerk, *and* the surgeon, dear Doctor.' Jack winked at Stephen. 'Then these scrubs sailed to La Guayra and *gave* her over to the Spaniards, who we were then at war with, of course. The ugliest thing I've ever seen in his Lordships' service.

'The Spaniards sailed her to Puerto Cabello, and that's where Ned Hamilton, who commanded our very own *Surprise* at the time, found her and cut her out in a fancy night manoevre that they still talk about to this very day. The *Surprises* killed any number of Spaniards, but most of the mutineers escaped. Many of them later went over to the U.S. Navy when France joined with Spain, and about a score of them were aboard, hoping to escape to the south seas. One of them, Haines, had offered to turn the King's evidence and peach the rest for his own pardon...'

'Informers--Lord, the world is full of them, so it is.' said Stephen.

'Yes, well, this one was scragged during this morning's engagement, and I intend to find the rest, starting with the two who dished this peach. But Stephen, I must confess I was hoping you would be able to help me. I need to separate them for their own good, and for ours. You wouldn't consider that informing, would you? I have a thoroughgoing description of each and every one at any rate, but since you would be examining all of the *Norfolks* eventually, I hoped you could perhaps make sure we hadn't missed any? In light of *Surprise's* history with this bunch, and our late terbations on this bloody island...this Haines won't be the last to lose the number of his mess unless we swiftly wet the fuse here. Won't you help me, Stephen?'

Stephen looked down at the papers Jack held across to him and read the first few names of the maledict litany:

'Seamus Baker, Sailmakers' Assistant. 27. 5 ft. 6 in. high. Strong-built, very much tatowed, and large crescent scar on left hand and wrist. Native of Guernsey and speaks French.

'George Bottenhorn, Waister. 39. 5 ft. 9 in. high. Broad-shouldered, Dutch extraction. Speaks bad English. Pronounced limp in gait. Marks from an issue on the back of his neck, and very much pitted with the small pox.

'James George, Able-bodied Seaman. 25. 5 ft. 6 in. Strong-made; sallow-complected, raw-boned. A scar where he has been stabbed in the belly.

'Patrick Harris, Midshipman. 27. 5 ft. 6in. high. Fair. Slender. Ochreish-haired, very freckled. Brother of Stephen. Port-wine birthmark on shoulderblade. One blue eye, in which he is blind.

'Stephen Harris, Able-bodied Seaman. 25. 5 ft. 8 in. high. Fair, but strong-made and long-limbed. Very much tatowed. Brother of Patrick.

'David Jonas, Foretop Captain. 27. 5 ft. 5 in. high. Slender built, strong, very well-made. Eyes green. Star tatowed on right shoulder. Has large scars on left ankle from grape.

'Robert MacEachern, Able-bodied Seaman. 23. 5 ft. 8 in. high. Stout shouldered, dark-complexion. A scar upon the left cheek and tatowed in several places. May have grown strong blackish beard.

'George McGuffin, Able-bodied Seaman. 32. 5 ft. 6 in. Dark, swarthy complexion. Eyes and hair very dark brown. Hands show mark of a severe scald. He is subject to Violent perspiration, especially in his hands, so that he soils anything he handles.'

Stephen laughed, and Jack raised his eyebrows.

'You laugh, Stephen, but believe me, these matters are of the utmost gravity to the navy...'

'Well, my dear, *gravitas* aside, the very crasis of these fellows is captured on the page here.' Stephen's eyes shifted from Jack back to the admiralties' colourful mutineer *résumés*.

Jack scrupled a sly smile. 'Well, Stephen, truth be told, I think we've gotten most of them already. But just in case one or two fell through the scuppers...you understand.'

'Of course I do, Jack, and if I do see any of these men I should think they would stand out like a crow in a blizzard.'

'Thankee, Stephen!' said Jack, putting the paper aside, then brightening: 'Do you think, Doctor, that we'll be able to have some music tomorrow evening? I haven't sawed my fiddle in weeks!'

In the hold of *Enderby*, within the makeshift compartment Mr. Lamb had created to hold the *Hermiones*, Patty Harris quietly whispered to Mr. Richards, the fellow prisoner to his right: 'I'll say this, Keith, the eating's much improved since we became prisoners of *Surprise*. I was so clemmed on that bloody rock.'

'You can fuck your bleedin' vittles and that accursed *Surprise* as well, Patrick Harris,' said Richards. 'She's dogged us since '99, and now this Goldilocks commanding her has cooked our stew, but good. *Thems* your vittles.'

'That's no way to talk to your elders, Keith,' said William Muspratt, who always tried to observe decorum, especially under trying circumstances such as these.

'Well, pardon me, Gov'nor, but I thought we was all on our way to a bleedin' hanging in Barbados,' snarled Richards.

'We're going to a Courts Martial,' said Harris.

'Oh, Lord, Pat, come on, man! You don't believe that now do you?' asked Richards.

'Well,' replied Harris with a chagrined sneer, 'No, as me old father used to say: "I dunna suspect it at 'tall, at 'tall", but we can'na let our chins drop just yet, now can we?'

'They call him "Lucky Jack Aubrey," this new captain of *Surprise*...' murmured Jonas, '...and luck he may need, mates.'

Harris grinned, 'It is a long fetch to Barbados, is it not Mr. Muspratt?'

Muspratt did not smile: ''Tis indeed, Mr. Harris, 'tis indeed.'

'Quiet down below!' yelled a marine guard, and the hold of *Enderby* grew silent again.

Chapter Two

At four bells in the morning watch Jemmy Ducks, at Killick's behest, had already milked Aspasia, the gun room goat, and was now fully engaged in tending the fowl pen aboard *Surprise* in preparation for this evening's repast.

By one bell in the forenoon watch Killick had already laid out the captain's uniform for a meal still eight hours away, so he decided to carefully clean the epaulet again. In the preceding day he had already polished to a beaming glow every brassen object in the cabin from the tell-tale compass to the gimballs on the weather glass.

But now he turned his attention to an old mark on a piece of furniture. The piece itself a curiosity of beautifully polished surfaces which opened up or folded together as a compact sort of... something. It was a gift to Doctor Maturin from his wife, Dianna Villiers, and he customarily left it in the captain's quarters for use as a music stand. A wonder of the cabinetry craft in more ways than one, but the unfortunate Lord Clonfert had left a ring-stain with a glass of claret not long before his untimely demise, and Killick had never been able to remove it since. Though he had cursed it many times, Killick never cursed the poor, late Lord Clonfert, but only because he didn't know it had been Clonfert's glass.

Today there would be no cursing. Today, uncharacteristically, Killick was free of his usual rancor, his coarse, cross-grained, willful, obstinate stupidity. This morning, as he ground the coffee beans with the pestle to prepare it in the Arabian fashion his captain and the doctor preferred, the return to the old routine has filled Killick with a deep, if ephemeral sense of contentment.

It was a sensibility profoundly shared by almost every man aboard. They all knew how tenuous their captain's situation had been on the island, but more than that, to the *Surprises* it now appeared *Surprise* had completely turned her fate around. Chance, as it turned out, had been with them all along. Their captain *was* 'Lucky' after all, and, it stood to reason, so were they. This voyage to the far side of the world had been marked from the outset when they shipped from Gibraltar with a parson, a jonah, and, to crown it, the bosun's black cat, Scourge, aboard. The subsequent contrary weather, the many severe blows and the refusal of the normal trades in general to cooperate, had worn down the whole crew. Then when the captain and ships' surgeon were lost overboard for days it truly seemed to confirm the most pessimistic premonitions among the superstitious.

But now, the parson, Mr. Martin, had won over the bulk of the crew with his chorale exercises, the jinx had been given a jonah's lift some weeks ago, and Scourge had disappeared, apparently eaten. Soon, they would weigh and begin the obversant voyage; with a prize in tow and no bad omens to worry sailors.

So Killick was content in his work, and so were the cook and Jemmy Ducks, and the loblolly boy, and everyone on deck this morning holystoning; a happy, busy, humming hive of a ship.

The mood remained so all afternoon, despite the great deal of work to be done by everyone, and it did nothing to lessen the mood when Jack gave the order at four bells for most of the hands to cease work and splice the main brace. By the time the dinghy arrived with Tanzi Jones and a youngster from *Enderby*, it seemed to Tanzi they were being welcomed aboard the happiest man o'war he could remember, outside of one engaged with a worthy prize, of course. He was shown to the companionway outside the gunroom where he found they were the first dinner guests to arrive. He pulled a quarter-fathom length of twiddling line from his pocket, held up the bitter end, and turned to his young companion.

'So, as I was saying, the whipping line gets turned in 'twixt the rope and its' own bight on every bend; do you see that, *bach*?' His nimble fingers braided two perfect rows of knotted whipping around the tip of the light hemp line. 'Now,' Tanzi held up a finger, 'Now we rove the whipping line through the rope, thus. Notice the end strand which already has the loop around it? Lift the snaking turn over its' top and pull the short end.' He handed the rope to the youngster: 'Here, now you braid up two more rows and finish it with a simple reef knot, and that's what I call a *working* West Country whipping. Don't braid too loose now, *bach*, nor too tight neither, mind, when you get a might stronger. It's a handsome whipping though, ain't it?

' 'Aye, Tanzi, the handsomest I've seen, to be sure,' he replied, 'But my mind is so aswim these days with whippings, knots, bends, hitches, and long-splices. I swear there's no room left in me brain to recall it all.'

'Well,' laughed Tanzi, 'you're *not* to swear, it's disrespectful, and you're going to have to grow a bigger brain soon anyway, before we start showing you the sailmaker's arts.'

'Well, no disrespect Tanzi, but if you was to assist me in my endeavors to share in some of tonight's victuals, maybe growing a larger brain ain't out of the question, eh?'

Tanzi's one remaining eye gleamed down at the lad and he smiled: 'A nod's as good as a wink, and Bob's-your-uncle, or so I'm told, *bach*.'

At that the other guests began to arrive, starting with Mr. Butcher, surgeon for *Norfolk*, followed promptly by Maitland, the officer of the watch, and Boyle, a young gentleman mate of the watch who tonight would be his server, due to the shortage of marines.

Presently the marine Oakes did arrive, but as Jack's escort. Captain Aubrey usually would eschew the use of his marine guard aboard *Surprise*, but under the present circumstances Jack felt it prudent. Half running down the companionway behind Jack came Stephen, his wig a bit askew, followed by the reverend, Mr. Martin.

'Welcome Captain,' said Wilkens, swinging open the gunroom door. The purser, Mr. Abrams, and Mr. Lamb arrived shortly with Lord Garrow's son, Mr. Blackeney, in tow to serve. Last to arrive were Mowett and Mr. Honey, whose server would be the poor squeaker Nesbit who's collar bone had finally mended after a fall from the ratlines.

Out of respect for the cloth, Jack seated the chaplain to his right with Stephen beyond him, then Abrams, Lamb, Honey, and Butcher at the far end and around to Jack's left where Mowett sat with Tanzi between himself and Maitland, and Gunner Wilkins on the far left.

Martin had just begun saying grace when Killick arrived with a stout black boy who helped him place a great massive lobscouse on the table. As he concluded his truncated incantation Martin's one eye seemed to glaze a bit, along with those of half the guests, and the room fell silent of speech as the assembled consumed two courses of the lobscouse, four three-decker goose pies Jemmy Ducks prepared, three and a half bushels of potatoes and pounded biscuit, three courses of pease pudding that arrived in dishes the size of dinghies, plus assorted frumenty, two juicy Strasburg pies, eighteen pounds of smoked tongue, and so on. After some time, Killick brought in the *piece de resistance* of the evening, a drown baby.

'Oh, a drown baby!' exclaimed Jack, who somehow appeared still to be hungry, 'It's one of my favourites.'

'Which it ain't spotted dog since the cook hadn't no currants, Sir,' said Killick. 'Oh, I told him, Sir: "The Captain's preferred dish is spotted dog," says I, but he said: "Nonetheless, without no currants it's a drown baby or it's naught" '

'It's fine, fine, thankee, Killick! And my very best compliments to the cook!' said Jack as he plunged his knife.

At last the cloth was withdrawn, and they drank the King, wives and sweethearts, and confusion to Buonaparte, and then Jack, pushing back his chair and easing his waistcoat, turned to his left and said: 'Mr. Mowett, a glass of wine with you, and pray, tell us something of your motions since *Surprise* was blown off.'

'Well Sir, to begin, Sir, as you know I did indeed gackle my cables as you ordered, Sir, but even with her kedged fore and aft as taut as I dared, plus a pair of handy billies abeam, still she swung 'round hard enough once that the cable hooked the cathead and snapped off a piece like it was cork. We knew we had to weigh before we broke a riding bitt, but even that was a cumbrous matter, with the rising sea. So when we got some seaway I was afraid to beat up with that fished mizzen--'

'I double-woulded it, but I couldn't get an whole new spar big enough,' interjected Lamb.

'Well,' Mowett smiled at Lamb, 'In a lighter blow it would have answered fine, I've no doubt, which was all the more reason not to let the cross jack carry away with it.'

'Sound judgement, Mr. Mowett.,' said Jack.

'Thankee, Sir. So, without no mizzen we was forced to scud as soon as we got sea room, and wait for the storm to clear.

'She spooned like that all night and morning under storm trys'ls and stays'ls, until just before noon when the weather eased enough to get a poor sighting, which I thought must be wrong, since we was almost ninety miles off the lee of that infernal Sodbury's Island out there! Naturally, and with all due haste we began the beat back up, and by noon the next day we realized our first fix was right after all, and it would still be a long fetch back.'

Mowett looked down for a moment, and then looked past Jack at Stephen. 'We was not a happy ship, having run widdershins all night, and what with all the worry over relations on the island, and the good Doctor's accident...' He looked across to Mr. Butcher, '...and his impending surgery...'

'As it turned out,' said Butcher, 'I was denied the chance to employ your excellent trephane tool, Dr. Maturin, though I assure you I've performed the procedure scores of times without mishap.'

Stephen, who despite his slight frame had held to the pace during dinner, now was perhaps leading the pace on the after-dinner Madeira. He sat with a somewhat saturnine slo-eyed expression of stupid complaisance. It crossed his mind that only yesterday he had been acutely ambivalent over Butcher's tending of Tanzi Jones, and now he was sanguine upon being reminded that this same, so to speak, 'Butcher,' not long ago nearly performed brain surgery on Stephen himself. But now that he was back aboard, Stephen once again had access to the calming effect of his judicious use of tincture of laudanum.

Stephen raised his glass and toasted Mr. Butcher's readiness, and Butcher in turn toasted Stephen's recovery, however disappointing it may have been for him privately.

'A glass of wine with you, Mr. Butcher!' said Jack, 'I've watched Doctor Maturin perform the bold procedure many times.' Jack had been unable to watch, however, when Butcher was preparing to minstrate to Stephen. 'Most recently he brought Joe Plaice back to life like Lazurus, and then plugged his skull with a three-shilling piece the armourer wrought flat; and both Mr. Mowett and Mr. Lamb were there in the year one, on the quarterdeck of dear old *Sophie*, when Doctor Maturin roused out Mr. Day's brains and put them back to rights, good as new. We were amazed! But Mr. Mowett, pray, finish your tale.'

'Well, Sir, the next four days there ain't much to report except beat and tack, watch-and-watch, with *Surprise* banging away, twisting like a corkscrew the whole while, and every hand that wasn't bending sail was either splicing, or putting up cordage, excepting the reefers, of course, which they was bobbing up and down the rigging like blue jays on Sunday.

'Shortly before sunset the foremast lookout bawled out a sail to the starboard bow. "Where away?" I says, and he said it had been just a point or two to starboard ahead, but hull down and very distant. With the next scend of *Surprise* he lost sight of her again, but he did think he spied a crows' nest and that got me thinking it was a whaler, and headed for Sodbury's, same as us, but,' Mowett smiled slyly, 'to what purpose? That was the question.'

All the officers at the table smiled as they recalled the galvanizing effect aboard a good fighting ship when a snow is first sighted, and pregnant with possibilities. Mowett turned to his left where Tanzi sat, 'We were nigh certain we hadn't been spotted.'

'I was under guard, of course,' said Tanzi, 'But they never changed sailing orders 'til the next day, and then they had a little trouble with old *Enderby's* quirks of sailing, so to speak. They missed stays twice, and all us old *Enderbys* was under guard in the waist, grinning like foxes the whole time and about to burst. But please, go on Mr. Mowett.'

'Well then, as I said the sun was setting when we spotted her, but I took careful lunar sightings that night, and we threw the log constantly. I reckoned that by altering course around midnight from west by north to west by sou'west we'd fetch the island by the next day, which we did as we all know!'

Tanzi raised his Madeira, 'A glass of wine with you, Mr. Mowett, for your fine figuring!'

Everyone laughed, including Butcher, and everyone drank a glass to Mowett's timoneerage, as he continued.

'I got the feeling every able-bodied jack was calculating shares out to the two-eighths of two hundred and fifty-six, so I thought the least I could do was get the ship's trigonometry right.'

'Well said, Mowett!' said Jack, and everyone laughed and drank again.

'But in truth, as you know, Sir, my aim was to beat up as far as possible and put the snow between *Surprise* and this blee--this bloomin' island, so whatever she turned out to be, *Surprise* would have the weather-gage.'

'Which you certainly did when we saw you! Ha-ha!' laughed Jack, and toasted another glass to *Surprise*, '...The finest windward sailing man o' war in His Majesty's Navy, I dare say!'

'Well, Sir,' continued Mowett, "It lightened very slowly at dawn, with showers drifting from nor'west to nor'east; as the light grew and the veil of rain parted to the sou'east, there she lay, hull up. I luffed the coarse to reduce our speed of approach, since it was obvious by how she sat in the water *Surprise* could outsail her. When we were three miles or so off I fired a gun to leeward and run up the 'Jack.'

'Did they amuse you, Mr. Mowett?' asked Jack.

'Oh, a bit, Sir. I think she wore a Russian burgee at first, then they gave something that looked like last months' signal, but when we was a good two miles away she put on more canvas and took a broad reach, hoping to outpace us. We did have to spread a great deal of canvas, as you saw, but of course they didn't know we was just racing them right up onto the shoal, anyways. Which I knew *Enderby* would let us know well in advance exactly where that reef was at that tide.'

The table drank a toast to the glorious capture, and Tanzi was about to propose a toast to *Enderbys'* still being afloat, though dismasted. But when he reached for his glass it was missing. He tried to discreetly turn around to his server, whom he knew to be heel-tapping this entire side of the table. However, it is very difficult to discreetly turn and nod, and actually quite impossible to wink, when one has only the one eye, as Tanzi now had. Tanzi hadn't necessarily wanted Captain Aubrey to catch his young protégé in the act, but now that he had, Jack thought he noticed something familiar about the boy. Just a flashing glimpse of some remembrance, some imagined recognition.

Jack turned to Tanzi and said: 'Our former master-at-arms, Mr. Allen, had some experience with whaling and told Mr. Martin here, and Stephen and myself some amazing stories before he was shipped as acting first of *Danae,* which we captured several weeks ago and sent off back 'round the Horn. Pray, tell us, how were you getting on before your capture by the Americans?'

'Well, Sir, we wasn't getting rich, that is to say we found no ambergris, nor pearls as big as Portsmouth, nor anything of that sort, but we was plyin' a respectable, decent amount, I suppose, though I ain't really a whaler. Still, it bothered me when the Americans burned their other prizes; right to the waterline, they did. Even *Intrepid Fox*, which was a right nice ship with a good ol' crew.'

'A practice I don't prefer myself. But tell me,' said Jack, 'are you by any chance familiar with the private yacht also called *Intrepid Fox*?'

'No, Sir,' Tanzi shook his head, 'yachting is a rich man's trifle.'

'Well, let me assure you there was nothing trifling about some of the wagering going on back in '92, when the Duke of Cresswell was said to have bet five hundred guineas on *Intrepid Fox* with her owner Connor Stennis at the helm, against Lord Buckley sailing his own *Chevisance*. In the event, conditions proved more favorable to *Chevisance*, but *Intrepid Fox* came straight at 'em, boarded, and cut their rigging, to win the day. Of course, they've made rules since outlawing all sorts of things, and I agree with you, Tanzi;

nowadays, yachting is trifling; too restricted to be enjoyable...man gets penalized for superior tactics... But please, continue, I'm afraid I interrupted your whaling tales, Tanzi.'

'Oh, I'm not really a whaler though, Sir, or at least I wasn't 'til this hitch, and I hope not to be again. I signed on strictly for the money, and to sail 'round the Horn, but flensing and me aboard ship don't agree. And killing them mighty fishes don't agree with me, *nor* the whales neither, I fear.'

This remark caused everyone at the table except Martin and Stephen to laugh, and Jack glanced over and noticed Tanzi's server was now furtively eating a piece of goose pie hidden in his pocket, and again Jack felt as if he'd seen the boy before somewhere.

'I understand the species called "finner" can be very dangerous to hunt, yes?' asked Stephen.

'Oh, any of 'em can raise quite the ruckus whenere' they're of a mind to, Doctor!' Tanzi leaned into the candlelight and the table grew silent. 'Have you ever been to Mocha Island, Doctor?'

'Stephen gave a pointed look and said: 'No, I have not, although not for lack of desire, sad to say. However, I have sailed *past* Mocha Island, as I also sailed *past* Juan Fernandez Island, and Diego Rivera Island, Lobos Island, Tristan de Cunha, and the Galapagos for all love, and a score of other fascinating places, while we made all speed, so as to end up here on Old Sodbury's Island.'

''Tis the curse of a natural philosopher aboard a man o' war I've found,' said Martin rather smugly, although it was Stephen himself had warned Martin that it was so.

'Well, Doctor,' said Tanzi, 'In the waters off the sou'west of Mocha Island is a finner the old timers talked about. He's been smashing longboats for at least ten years now. They know him by a big white spot on his head, and they call him Mocha Dick. Just last season he put a hole in the stern of *Woodagar* so big with his fluke she sank in ten minutes. Two launch crews escaped with their lives to tell the tale, and there's been other ships turn up missing in previous years, still unaccounted for, and all the whalers blame Mocha Dick. Since the *Woodagar*, the Dutch have offered a reward of two hundred guilders for the blubber of Mocha Dick, but I've yet to meet the whaler who's interested in the job.'

'So, you see there, Stephen?' joked Jack, 'Perhaps it's all for the best that we've raced past all these vile places, doing the King's duty.'

Stephen feigned chagrin, for he was far too happy after such a satisfying meal, and so much fortifying spirits, for genuine chagrin. 'I don't suppose we'll be any more likely to visit some of these spots on our peripatetic return, will we, Jack?'

'Well,' said Jack, 'of course we haven't a moment to lose, and we must get *Enderby* back...but on the other hand, we'll have to water at least once somewhere this side of the Horn, and we may need more provisions by then as well, though I doubt it after seeing *Enderbys'* stowage; but one never knows.' Jack smiled at his friend, 'What a pity we're encumbered with His Majesty's duties, else what a splendid yacht *Surprise* would be for your natural philosophy explorations, Doctor.'

'It has often occurred the same to me,' said Stephen, who really wasn't joking.

Tanzi's server was pouring him a bumbo of rum and Jack said: 'Tell me, Tanzi, who is this young gentleman you brought with you tonight?'

'Oh, he's an aspiring young gentleman, Sir. Young Nic here is coming up through the hawse-holes, so to speak, Sir.'

Jack turned to the youngster who was standing respectfully, if somewhat nervously and awkwardly, due to the biscuits secreted under his jacket. 'What's your name young man?' and again Jack had an eerie sense of familiarity with his face as the lad began to speak and subtle expression flitted across his countenance.

'My name's Nicodemus Crofter, Captain Aubrey...' and suddenly Jack's face lit up.

'Of *course* that's your name--"Nicodemus" you say?--Crofter. Surely your father must be Ronald Crofter, is he not?'

Nic sputtered a bit and nodded his head, and Jack continued: 'The resemblance is astonishing. Your father and I were both master's mates on *Romulus* in '88, with Captain Broke.'

'Beggin' pardon, Sir,' asked Wilkens, 'the same Captain Broke who defeated *Chesapeake* in Boston last year?'

'Yes indeed, Mr. Wilkens,' nodded Jack, 'Broke was always

a great one for gunnery practice you know, but unfortunately, he was so badly wounded in his engagement with *Chesapeake*, I doubt he'll be able to command another ship.'

Jack looked again at Nic. 'But what a grand passage home your father and I had on the *Romulus.'* Jack also remembered an incident long ago in which Ronald Crofter had shielded him from an over-zealous press-gang by posing as Jack, and then almost miraculously producing a letter of exemption, forged by Crofter of course, and sent the press gang away quite crest fallen. But it would never do for Jack, a post captain after all, to relate such a story here, however relaxed discipline may be tonight.

'I hope your father has enjoyed good fortune since he left the Navy, Nic.'

'Oh, yes Sir, He left the Navy to help my grandfather, his da', with the channel trade. He said he had no real interest with the Admiralty or government, so he might never make post anyway.'

Jack thought ruefully of his own father, the worst snollygoster in Parliament, whose radical views had certainly never helped Jack's navy career. 'So he's still sailing then, is he?' asked Jack.

'Oh, yes, Sir. All around the North Sea, the Wadden Sea, and the Bay of Biscay, an' which he says is as bad a patch of sea as any blue water sailor's.'

'The Bay of Biscay?' asked Jack, 'I've seen it as black as the Earl of Hell's riding boots, and blowing like Purgatory with the lid off. I'm afraid the Admiralty lost a good commander in your father; what a capital, splendid fellow I remember him as, and how happy I am to meet his son. And do you know what has become of his particular friend, Mr. Guiness? He served as a mid on *Romulus* with us.'

'Oh, Mr. Guiness, Sir?' replied Nic, 'Well, he tried his hand in the theatric' trades, Sir, and put every farthing he had into it. Not that he could afford to stage the most stylish of plays, but he always tried to provide cheap entertainment. Sad to say, he lost everything to projectors and had to give up his playhouse to the bankers.'

This remark unwittingly pierced Jack, momentarily bringing to mind his own small fortune from his successful Mauritius campaign being rapidly dissipated this very minute back at Ashgrove cottage, but he only said: 'Projectors...blasted projectors.'

Quickly returning to his cheerful self, Jack said to Nic: 'Thankfully, we've no projectors at sea, but our fair share of poets, ha-ha!'

'Very well stated, Jack, my compliments,' said Stephen, 'you're perhaps something of a poet yourself, you are.'

'Jack turned to Tanzi and said: '*Surprise* is very lucky that we often have two poets aboard; Mr. Rowen, who's currently aboard *Danae* with Allen, and Mr. Mowett here, who is a crew favourite, fore and aft of the mast.'

'How very nice of you to say so, Sir,' said Mowett, by no means a vain man, but a man, nonetheless, of transparent false modesty when it came to his poetry.

'Would you care to favour us with one of your poems,' asked Jack.

'Well, Sir, I was just putting the finishing touch, so to speak, to a little poem I call: "Becalmed in the Middle Watch."'

'Please proceed, Mr. Mowett.'

Mowett stood up as erect as one could in *Surprises*' gunroom and began:

'"Becalmed in the Middle Watch,"
'Round middle watch the fair sough fell,
So still it damped the Boson's bell.
The mate said: "Mind our steerage way,
Or pull the sweeps 'til break o' day."

Then he took good measure with a will and might,
He could take no pleasure in the starlit night,
As he squinted 'round in a focused gawk,
'Cross a glassy sea where no kittens walked.
'Cross a fishmonger's slab of a glassy sea,
Of a colour drab, of yesterday's tea.

Their hempen fibres clasped in prayer,
T'gallants combed the torpid air,
To find a puff upon to play,
While sailors scratched her old backstay.

Then from the masthead:
"Zephyr! Zephyr! There, I say!"
Then from the Master:
"Zephyr? Zephyr? Where away?"
"Four points off the starboard bow,
And moving toward us even now!"

"Then bend the spanker, 'mates we're blest,
"The airs just took a midnights' rest." '

'Very clever turn, Mr. Mowett,' said Jack. 'How I wish I were such a prodigious hand with the King's English, and could put words to such purpose. Very clever..,' he said again with genuine admiration, and they all had a glass to Mowett's poem, and another to the foremast lookout.

"Tell me,' Tanzi asked the nascent poetry corner, 'have you all heard the one called: "Duke William?" '

'There's a poem about His Majesty's third son?' Turning to Stephen and Martin, Jack explained: 'William, you remember, entered into service as a midshipman and rose to rear admiral.'

'He's Duke of Clarence, is he not?' asked Martin, 'I should like very much to hear it. Do you know it, Mr. Jones?'

'Well, I'll try,' said Tanzi, though I can't remember much of it. It's a dance really; a waltz it is, but I'll try to recall it.'

Tanzi stood up, curiously formal suddenly, and with his hand over one breast like a statue of Demonsthanes giving a great allocution, he began:

'"Duke William"

Duke William and a nobleman,
Heroes of England's nation,
Got up one morn by two o' clock,
To take a recreation.

Unto the suburbs they did go,
In sailor's dress from top to toe;
Then Duke William said : "Let us know,

What usage have poor sailors?"

Before the sun had quite sunk out,
A press-gang that was bold and stout,
Portside streets they searched about,
To find out the bold sailors.

To a tender they did hail them;
The Captain he did meet, sir.
The Duke replied: "Kind gentleman,
Be mindful of your sheep, Sir."

With that the Captain he did say:
"I am your shepherd, I declare!
I'll let you know you saucy bear,
Go down amongst the sailors.

For your sauce, you saucy are,
We're sure to have you flogged sir."
Unto the gangway they did haul him,
To strip him like a dog , sir.

"Come strip," they cried. The Duke replied:
"I don't like your laws by far, Sir
I ne'er will strip for to be whipped,
So strip me if you dare, Sir." '

At this Wilkens ejaculated: 'That's tellin' 'em, Billy!' and Abrams, who could no longer contain himself finally burst out with: 'Oh, this blackgaurd don't know it's the old Dukey. He'll settle your hash, but good, he will!'

Lamb broke in and said: 'Let the man finish, you scrubs,' and then to Jack: 'Beggin' your pardon, Sir,' and Tanzi continued:

'"I ne'er will strip for to be whipped,
So strip me if you dare, Sir."

Then instantly the boatswain's knife,
Began for to undress, Sir

And instantly he did espy,
A star upon his breast, Sir.

Then on bended knees did fall,
And straight for mercy they did call.
The Duke replied: "Base villains, all
For using these poor sailors.

No wonder that my father can't
Get men to manage shipping,
For using these poor sailors so
And always them a-whipping;
But for the future sailors all
Shall have good usage great and small."

The sailors all with one huzza
Cried: "Heavens bless Duke William."

He ordered all new officers
That stood in need of wealth, sir,
And left the jolly crew some gold
That they might drink his health, sir.
They left the boat and sailed away,
The sailors all cried : "Bless the Day
On which was born Duke William!" '

'Capital, simply capital!' Enthused Jack when Tanzi sat down. 'Of course, William wasn't pressed, or anything of the sort, but not to pettifog, it don't signify where a good poem is concerned. And I agree with the spirit of the thing. As Nelson used to say: "Aft the mast the more honor, before the mast the better man." '

'Nelson said that, did he, Jack?' asked Stephen.

'On more than one occasion; he could be a deep file at times.'

Abrams, Honey, and Maitland had left after the poetry and at last Tanzi and Nic had to bid their farewells and return to *Enderby*. Wilkens was thanked heartily and the guests gradually filed out.

Jack and Stephen had repaired to Jack's quarters for music, but both Stephen's violin cello and Jack's violin were so badly out of tune initially that they played once poorly through Correlli's C Major and were both exhausted. They made their respective apologies, and agreed there seemed every chance they would have more time for music on this return voyage, if all went well.

Down in *Enderbys'* hold Richards nudged Jonas: 'They finally quit their sawin', I believe.'

'Oh,' whispered Jonas, 'Is that what it was? I thought the rats was fighting over midshipman's nuts in the galley.'

'Well,' said Richards, 'I say: "Fiddle away, Nero," we'll ship your rudder, we will. "Lucky Jack Aubrey," why I've heard better fiddle on capstan shantys.'

'Luck he may need, mates; luck he may need...' said Jonas again.

Chapter Three

The equatorial dawn arrived with its customary abruptness: the keen edged meniscus of the deep blue Pacific met a fine-drawn arc of lofty blue sky, while due east a perfectly round sun emerged hull-up, and silently began its' quotidian ascent. Beams of effulgent yellow light spread westward and they reflected off the white surf that broke along the high cliffs of Old Sodbury's Island. Jack stood on the windward quarterdeck with his breakfast tray of cullops and toasted cheese resting on the taffrail, and gazed west toward the gibbous setting moon, while *Surprises*' barge, both cutters, the gig, the pinnace, and even the jolly boat clustered about *Enderby*.

'Good morning, Stephen,' he said as the ship's surgeon arrived a bit later than usual. 'The rain has stopped at last, and not a moment too soon; shall I have Killick bring you some toasted cheese? I've still a pot or two of Ashgrove cottage marmalade as well, and it's quite delicious...'

'No, thank you, Jack,' said Stephen, 'I'm afraid I'm feeling a bit crapulous this morning; too much toasting last night, so to say. Just coffee if you will.'

'You do look a bit green about the gills, Doctor. Perhaps

you should take some of your own physic,' teased Jack, 'but such a feast is worth a bit of regret, is it not?'

'Well,' said Stephen slowly, 'I'll say that since I awoke I've carried a part of Mowett's catching little poem 'round in my head. And the dear knows the whole evening was quite the grand plethoric rush of plenitude after all of our privations, was it not? Sure, I'll be just fine by noon, I will.'

'I'll be fine when *Enderby* swims,' said Jack, 'and this bloody island is astern of us. *Enderby* ran aground for the whole stock and fluke of her. That is to say, she really put her keel into it, so to speak, and with that globous moon over there,' Jack waved his coffee toward the moonset, 'I'd say we've got two more days in which to free her before we have to wait for the next spring tide and be here for another fortnight.'

'Moses in the mountains! Perish the thought, Jack!' said Stephen in real alarm, 'Why then on earth aren't they working on it right now?'

'It won't answer right now, tide is out. Right now as you can see, we're unloading her of as much heavy cargo as possible. Then, this afternoon around sunset at slackwater we'll try to kedge her off. But before then I aim to restep the fore and maintop masts and refit the mizzen shrouds; if we can get sails on her, that could help pull her off as well.'

'May Mary and Patrick help you,' said Stephen.

By five bells in the second dog watch only *Enderbys'* foremast had been restepped and the mizzen standing rigging partly refit, and some, but not most, of her cargo was off-loaded onto the small fleet of now over-laden ships' boats lying to in the placid lagoon. The capstan crew, made up almost entirely of *Enderbys*, sang out *All Aboard For Cuckolds Reach* and bent to their task, causing the *Surprises*, all man o' war's men of course and unaccustommed to shantys, to stop whatever they were engaged in to listen to the unfamiliar songs.

In the doing the kedge anchor failed to hold twice, the first time wickedly snapping loose, resulting in two men injured. Stephen, who was sitting in *Surprises'* larboard chains with a lookout's glass, watched the work with growing concern as high tide approached.

And as he watched he saw all the men on deck running from one side of the ship to the other, starboard to larboard or perhaps *vice-versa*, Stephen could never remember. Again all together in a tight cluster, they ran all the way from one rail to another, all of a single bunch. Suddenly Stephen thought he saw *Enderby* sluice astern a foot or two. The slack in the cable was kedged in, and again everyone crowded together on deck and ran to and fro in a fashion that seemed somewhat jerky and astonishingly fast to Stephen as he watched through the glass. *Enderby* listed a bit and this time she slid back and clearly swam. A loud cheer went up from *Enderby* as she unrucked her fore course and wore some distance off the reef, where she hove to, and Jack gave the order to splice the main brace.

Jack came back across in the jolly boat under moonlight and immediately sent word for Stephen to come to his quarters for music, were he so inclined.

'Tell me,' asked Stephen when he arrived at Jack's cabin, 'why all the capers on *Enderby*? The running forth and back? Is that some part of naval ritual, or some sort of shamanism? Whatever it was, it seemed to answer.'

'Oh, we were cutting capers, I assure you, Stephen, ha-ha!' laughed Jack. 'We were sallying, actually; trying to rock the ship to-and-fro a bit to get her off the shoal.'

'Well, it is a most amusing technique, Jack,' said Stephen, 'and thank the dear it answered.'

'Yes,' said Jack, 'very happy about it myself. Tomorrow we'll weigh and we shall leave this dreadful little island for good.'

Both men sighed, and then Jack, holding his bow aloft, said: 'Shall we try the Correlli in C Major again, Doctor?' and the cabin filled with music, this time played in tune.

Surprise was underway before noon with *Enderby* astern commanded by Bonden. Shortly after their departure a very fresh gale from the southwest created a current and wind that made progress in the right direction impossible, and for the next two days they held to a course of north-by-east and waited for a sea change. Presently, Mr. Mowett and Captain Aubrey sat in the captains' quarters looking over several charts spilling off Jack's table.

'The thought occurs to me again,' said Jack as he peered

out the stern windows through the thick downpour and across the rainswept waters back toward Old Sodbury's Island, 'That by and large, taking one thing and another, I have never known any commission with so much weather in it, not even on the horrible old *Leopard.*'

'The *Leopard,*' said Mowett, then absently adding: '...the horrible old *Leopard.* It does seem that every day and night aboard her was a hard blow and filled with disaster, don't it? But at least the normal trades and currents weren't so contrary.'

'Contrary is the word to be sure, Mr. Mowett,' said Jack. 'We're literally going north instead of south, and if our easterly progress were any less, we'd be westerly. And even if we could make progress in *Surprise* against this wind, which we can't, we'd still have to contend with *Enderby* and this bizarre reversal of the seasonal currents.'

'This kind of heavy airs has got to blow itself out soon in these latitudes,' said Mowett, not really sure he believed it himself.

The rain stopped before first light and after an hour of improbably powerful variable gusts the wind lenified, and it might have looked to a landsman for a short while as if Mowett had been right. The sunrise was a crimson wonder which even Honey, who had had the middle watch, had stayed topside to witness, but like the other sailors on deck, to witness with distinct apprehension.

The swell, in so far as it was a vast regular up and down, certainly diminished, yet even Stephen, lying there awake in the morning, felt a strange uneasy motion that was a quick sudden kind of lurching with no decided direction, very unlike the ship's normal motions. It had obviously been going on for some considerable time, since there was a good deal of water washing about in his cabin, and his shoes were afloat.

'Padeen,' he called several times; and after a listening pause, 'where is that black rascal, his soul to the Devil?'

'God and Mary be with you, gentleman,' said Padeen, opening the door and sloshing the water.

'God and Mary be with you,' said Stephen, 'and Patrick.'

Padeen pointed upwards through the decks and said in English, 'The Devil's abroad.'

'I dare say he is,' said Stephen.

As he made his way topside Stephen was nearly flung backwards off a ladder, and arriving found Jack and most all of the starbowlins on deck. Aspasia came and nuzzled his hand like an anxious dog: a sudden jerk nearly had him over, but he saved himself by clapping onto her horns.

'Hold on, Doctor,' called Jack from the windward rail, 'the barky's a bit skittish today.'

'Pray, what does all this signify?' asked Stephen.

'Something of a blow,' said Jack, and smiling, nodded to the sky.

The horizon all around was of a blackish purple and over the whole sky there rolled great masses of cloud of a deep copper colour, moving in every direction with a strange unnatural speed; lightening flashed almost continuously in every part and the air was filled with the tremble of enormous thunder, far astern but traveling nearer. There was a steep sea, bursting with a tremendous surf as if under the impulsion of a very heavy gale: in fact the breeze was now no more than moderate. Yet in spite of it's moderation it was strikingly cold and it whistled through the rigging with a singularly keen shrilling note.

The t'gallantmasts had already been struck down on deck and all hands were now busy securing the boats on the booms with double gripes, sending up preventer stays, shrouds, braces and backstays, clapping double-breechings onto the guns, covering the forehatch and scuppers with tarpaulins and battening them down.

Jack went to his cabin to put some notes in the log and noticed that the glass was lower than he had ever seen it. By the time he returned on deck *Surprise* was under bare trees and all the yards were struck and stowed, when suddenly the air went absolutely still. The oily sea glassed off to huge long swells of a strange mustard green colour, and hung all around everything was a dense silence. Jack looked north and could see short seas a mile or two off and the sky momentarily brightened, Jack spun round to the south and saw the distant sky suddenly darken all across the horizon, and then darken further accompanied by a thick, utterly silent, yellow bolt of lightening that plunged into the southern sea.

'Christ's blood!' cursed Jack, and turning to Honey, 'Get every man below or else lashed to the mast immediately! There's not a moment to lose.'

Jack tried to call across to *Enderby* with a speaking horn, but the dormiant airs seemed to mute the very sound of his voice and his words fell noiselessly into the sea.

Stephen, who had insisted upon staying on deck, albeit lashed to the mizzen by an adamant Mowett, was enjoying the chance to view the horizon all around from the deck, without sails blocking the view. A lot of good it was doing him, he thought, when he noticed that there wasn't a single seabird in the entire sky. Then he looked south where a very strange sky was forming.

'Well, Doctor,' said Jack from the quarterdeck, 'I didn't think you were the type to enjoy a good blow, but this one could make you Mr. Butcher's patient again if you're not careful.'

'What blow are we speaking of?' asked Stephen, 'The air is still as a chapel, though I do see some queer clouds over there.'

'Well, Stephen, prepare yourself, because I think this is going to be the blow to bear the bell away. I hope *Enderby* don't sink, she swims so poor as she is.'

It was perfectly quiet for a minute, and then there was a faint, very faint, sibilous sound. At first it seemed all around, then it seemed to come from the north, but as it rapidly grew more audible it was clearly now coming from the south, where the sky was now ebony and a band of the sea in the extreme distance turned very black and was getting wider and closer. Within seconds the sound grew to a high-pitched, deafening, ear-splitting hiss, then lowered pitch as dense hail the size of birds' eggs engulfed both ships and the sea all about them, and began to pelt *Surprise* and make her hull and *Enderbys'* plangent like a pair of tympanum.

The hail fell hard for half of an hour as the rain increased and the wind and sea rose rapidly. There was a resounding thunderclap and the very fabric of the atmosphere seemed shredded as now blinding rain drown everything.

In the drenched hold of *Enderby*, Bonden had *Norfolks* manning the pumps almost non-stop, while he considered which cargo to throw overboard. Tanzi reported five feet of water in the well, and laden with this much cargo and so many prisoners, it wouldn't take a large mistake to scuttle her. Despite their propinquity the ships completely lost sight of each other for over an hour, but during a momentary shift each saw that they were still within three cable lengths or so.

On *Surprise* Jack had a large piece of the old blown-out mizzen rigged with a hawser line to trail astern to the south and impede *Surprises'* drift in the powerful current, but it's effect was in doubt and he was afraid it might foul the rudder so he had it hauled in, the southern gale all the while nearly lofting the men right off the deck as they clapped on for dear life.

The heavy weather held for all that day and night and, if possible, worsened as the swell seemed to gain momentum. Both ships remained watch-and-watch, four men at the wheel, pumps going in around the clock shifts, with St. Elmo at play all through the middle watch along the lower masthead.

A coruscatious stroke of lightening lit up *Enderby* for an unequal series of parsed seconds just as clearly as if it were day, and the wheel immediately reported a loss of control, whose cause proved to be the fusing of the pintle to the top gudgeon. This meant *Enderby* would have to be towed, but while just rigging an unwieldy towline in this pitching swell would be extremely cumbrous, hailing *Surprise* was impossible through the streaming slanting blackness, and signaling with *Enderby's* one deck gun would not answer because her powder was wet. The marines refused to squander their ordinance since their rifles couldn't be heard by *Surprise* anyway, and it wouldn't do to have the many prisoners observe whose flints, among the few marines, would fail in this penetrating dank.

Six hours later when the rain finally lifted for a moment neither ship was in sight of the other, *Enderby* having taken an errant bimble to the northwest. Fortunately, at the noon reading conditions had lessened so much that Bonden, aboard *Enderby*, had a Pakenham's rudder shipped, unfurled her foretops'l and cross jack, and had put her helm up for as easterly as this ungainly rig would allow, which Tanzi dubbed: 'Hove-to steerage.'

Meanwhile Jack had been pacing the seventeen yards back-and-forth along *Surprises'* windward quarterdeck since *Enderby* went missing. He considered that if she's sunk, surely Bonden would have gotten at least one or two of the boats away, but the weather, this particular weather, was so severe Jack knew anything was possible. He'd given his best glass, a splendid achromatic five lens Dollond, to Sims who went to the crosstrees, while Jack scoured the sea for flotsam. No wreckage was spotted, but no cargo either, so if she went down it must have been very fast, which wouldn't seem to agree with being struck by lightening, the last anyone had seen of her. If she were adrift, of course, Jack knew she must drift nowhere if not northwestly, and he had loaned Bonden one of *Surprises*' pair of superb Arnold chronometers, so if Barret could get a reading he, at least, would certainly know where *Enderby* was: and in the first dogwatch she was spotted, waddling off the larboard bow to the west-northwest, still all laden.

'Clear for starbowlins only gunnery practice, Mr. Mowett,' said Jack, snapping his glass shut, 'and have the target raft pulled well due east, will you? So nobody gets the wrong idea and tries to sink *Enderby*.'

Practice commenced poorly, with several guns, including old stalwarts Jumping Billy and Willful Death balking due to wet touch holes. However, by the end of the drill the *Surprises*' were cracking off broadsides in two minutes, twenty, which pleased Jack extremely, although it was only the one side. Before they reached *Enderby* the guns were breeched and the bulkheads refit, and a huge splice was readied in what would be the tow line.

The swell had dropped as the trawline of eight inch cable was passed between crews, accompanied by teasing persiflage as regards how was it *Enderby* was all of a ways out here? And in reply the question how was it it took *Surprise* so long to find them, big as life as they are, after all?

'Light along,' said Jack as the *Surprises* secured their end around the mizzen mast, and then turning to the men lowering the cable into the cutter, 'Handsomely, handsomely...'

The cable was bent to *Enderby's* riding bitt after being rove through the hawse holes to prevent the tow line pushing *Enderby's* bow any further downward; no need to slow *Surprise's* 'progress' anymore than necessary, and if the weather blew up again Jack was very afraid that, laden as she was, with her nose pulled downward she could pearl and broach-to.

'Well done,' said Jack, as he and Mowett looked astern down the cable toward *Enderby*, 'That was easy as kiss my hand. But we're barely making headway enough to taut the towline.'

'The last time I saw this sky in these latitudes just north of the line we hit a long spell of the doldrums,' said Mowett.

'I fear you're right, Mr. Mowett,' said Jack, 'but whilst we've yet air for making way, set a course north by east for now. We'll be sure not to head back into that red hell of a blow, and it will give me time to talk to Mr. Abrams and Mr. Ward regarding victualing. Then I'll take a hard look at the charts before we begin our next ambit, but I think our current position is going to dictate a rather unexpected turn from our original plans.'

'Before we begin the music this evening, Doctor, I wonder if I could ask you to step in here for a moment.' Jack beckoned Stephen from the great cabin, where they usually played, to the coach and shut the door behind them. 'Pray, step over this way if you will, Stephen,' said Jack, very quietly walking around the single carronade that was kept there and noiselessly placing two chairs from the dinner table behind the lower portion of the mizzenmast.

Stephen sat looking at his friend a bit puzzled but said nothing; Jack Aubrey, when he was afloat at least, was always a reasonably discreet person, but he was rarely furtive or gravely confidential as now.

'You will recall,' began Jack, *sotto voce*, 'a certain great responsibility we assumed while aboard *Danae*...some certain paperwork?'

Of course Stephen knew immediately he referred to a certain metal case they had removed from it's hiding place in the hold of the packet: it had accidentally burst open revealing its' contents to be for the most part large amounts of bank notes; very large amounts. Stephen had an instinctive aversion from the very beginning of his avocational career to the mixing of money with intelligence work, his own motivations being not pecuniary but primarily a loathing of Buonaparte. It had distressed him greatly when his suspicions of the true contents were confirmed to him. Stephen had counted it; more confirmation. Here was an amount of money so unspeakably large, it could only be intended to undermine and/or politically seize the reins of a nation. He had resealed it, pressing his curiously engraved watchkey into the cooling wax as a signet, and then given it over to Jack and tried to put it from his mind. He now answered with a silent nod to Jack.

'Well,' began Jack, speaking close to Stephen's ear, 'The situation is this: we must water at least once more before doubling, preferably somewhere we could also get tobacco, sugar, and something against the scurvy. But I came across a troubling little margin notation in *Enderby's* log written by her old captain saying they'd spoke a Russian whaler, *Karaginskly*, thirty-one days out of Valparaiso, where apparently things are a bit at sixes and sevens. That countryman of yours, Bernardo O'Higgins has been kicking up a great deal of sand as of late, put the whole political climate ahoo–'

'Countryman of mine?'

'A poor jest, forgive me, Stephen, but at any rate he is an unusually troublesome fellow regardless his country of origin. I believe he was borne of a native Chiléan, actually, his father being the Irish one, but he schooled in England and evidently not to the desired effect since he's just been named Commander of the rebel forces against Spain. An earthquake struck Valpariaso six weeks ago and the rebels have taken advantage of the situation to disrupt and loot as much shipping as possible.'

'Surely then, Jack, you're not thinking of risking a stop there?' asked Stephen.

'Oh, never in life, Doctor, nor anyplace else in Chilé I'm afraid,' said Jack, 'which is a shame, really, Valpairiso being the best port in the country, or the whole west coast of South America I should say, and with our current friendly relations with Spain...'

'However evanescent they should prove to be,' added Stephen, who, though Irish on one side of his illegitimate birth, was Catalán on the other, and as such despised the Spanish, which is to say Castilian, domination of Catalonia.

'That's the chafe of it, you see?' Jack knit his eyebrows from one side to the other. 'On the other hand, the vicissitudes of weather thus far have already contrived to place us north of the line, which makes the necessity of watering that much more certain and the question of just where rather nettlesome, fettered as we are with *Enderby* and that pestiferous box, I can't just go sailing blindly into a questionable political climate like an ordinary man o' war might. It would be like counting your hatchlings...no, rather it would be like trying to count all the eggs in one basket...like trying to count...?'

'Before they've hatched?' prompted Stephen.

'No, no. It's something about baskets and eggs, but I fear my tongue has brought me up on a lee shore again, Stephen, but you smoke my meaning, do you not?

'Completely. *Res ipso loquotor.*'

'Beg pardon?' asked Jack.

'The thing speaks for itself,' smiled Stephen, 'and perhaps the less spoken of the better, but what shall we do then, Jack?'

'I've not a decent chart for Columbia, and the same goes for the entire American isthmus; there are no known safe ports of any size, and even if there were it would be too far easterly. There's an ancient shipyard in Navidad, New Spain, something of a *dernier ressort*, but many years ago now pirates seized it and burned the boatyard, and I've no reason to believe the situation has improved.'

'It's perplexing to be sure,' said Stephen, 'but how can I help?'

'I may very well need your diplomatic skills, and most certainly I'll need your good Spanish, as I've decided to head for the only other decent bay available, San Diego, in the Californias,' said Jack.

'San Diego? Lord, that is rather far. It's northern California is it not, Jack?'

'Well, yes and no. It's on the very boundary of Alta and Baja California, but yes, it is around thirty degrees north,' said Jack, who smiled at Stephen's expression. 'They are under Spain, of course, although I understand a ship's welcome can depend on the whim of the local authorities on any given day.'

'I shall be more than happy to assist if possible,' said Stephen, 'Is that all there is to it then?'

'As far as I know so far,' said Jack, as they both rose and

returned to the great cabin, 'Not many English ships have made port there, so the reaction is unpredictable.'

Jack placed a sheet down and said: 'I wonder if we may try this Scarlotti tonight.'

While one part of Stephen played the Scarlotti, the greater part of his euphorous mind was pregnant with possibilities of the Californias. He said again silently to himself: 'The Californias! The grizzly bear! The buffalo! All the known great peregrines, and perhaps one waiting to be given its' name...and the Sea of Cortez; Mr. Allen had described it *aswim* with turtles!' Stephen decided however to attempt to restrain his expectations this time, to avert the sort of bitter disappointments that marked the first half of this trip.

Over the next days the ship at last began to fall into something of the steady routine of equatorial blue-water sailing: The sun, rising a bit astern now of the starboard beam and a little hotter every day, dried the freshly holystoned decks the moment it arrived and then beheld the ordered sequence of events--hammocks piped up, hands piped to breakfast, berth-deck cleaned and aired, Jamie Pratt, the loblolly boy, tending the sickbay breakfast, the hands piped to the great-gun exercise or reefing topsails or to beautifying the ship, the altitude observed, the ship's latitude and progress determined, noon proclaimed, hands piped to dinner, the ceremony of the mixing of the grog by the master's mate -- three of water, one of rum, and due proportions of lime juice and sugar -- the drumbeat one hour later for the gunroom meal, then the quiet afternoon, with supper and more grog at six bells, and quarters somewhat later, the ship cleared for action and all the hands at their fighting stations -- although usually now, to conserve powder, Jack only ran the guns in and out, a helpful drill perhaps, but Jack much preferred the bang and jump of the genuine discharge to prepare men for battle, to say nothing of teaching them to point the muzzle in the right direction.

Sailing in light airs with t'gallants and royals set, Jack was towing the ship's boats now as well as *Enderby* to keep the hulls cool and seaworthy, yet as noon readings were taken the tar still bubbled up through the oakum in the poop deck. Stephen had bled the crew and vainly bemoaned as he always did the drinking of far too much grog in the middle latitudes. Aboard *Enderby* especially there was mould everywhere now, and everything had to be stored and aired with great care, as they awaited the Humbolt current to nudge them along, and perhaps provide an occasional fresh following breeze.

One afternoon Jack called down from the quarterdeck to Mr. Blackeney: 'My compliments to Doctor Maturin, and pray, ask him if he could join me at his first convenience.'

The Doctor and Martin were happily rapt in a careful organization of Stephen's collection of Brasilian coleoptera when Blackeney arrived with the rather mandatory invitation, and Stephen reluctantly trudged his way to the quarterdeck where *Surprise* was wearing a mountain of canvas in the light airs: all her staysails and jibs, the spritsail, and aloft the royals, skysails and skyscrapers.

'Hello Stephen!' said Jack, 'I wanted you to see this --you may very well never get another chance.'

'What possible earthly thing could it be then, Jack?' Stephen's imagination began to peruse through a catalog of the bizarre, the singular, the anomalous; he had a taste for the bizarre and often found it on these sea voyages.

Jack looked aloft, and Stephen did the same, searching for a bird now. 'Do you see it up there?' asked Jack.

'No I don't,' replied Stephen, looking up through his dark blue spectacles, squinting up and blinking in the bright glare of the sails.

'The sail, Stephen, the sail!' said Jack, gesturing skyward as Stephen stood shielding his face with his hand, 'Do you not see it? Not the triangular kite sail, we have used that before this; I mean the square kite sail aloft of it.'

Stephen looked quizzically at Jack.

'Do you see, Stephen, it's a *moonraker*, or as some used to call them, a "stargazer" sail, I daresay if you sail another ten years you may never see one employed again!'

The reason for Jack's clearly evident delight in this escaped Stephen entirely, but not the delight itself, and he found himself at a loss; at first he feigned interest until it occurred that if he were to be overly graceful in his appreciation it would almost certainly mean many more such interruptions in the future.

The water's temperature was a wonderfully refreshing handful of degrees cooler than the air and one of the great pleasures came in the afternoons, with the ships largely becalmed, most of the people plunged over the side, most into a shallow swimming-bath made of a sunken sail but some into the open sea itself, for no sharks had been seen since they left Old Sodbury's, at least none that followed the ship. Whenever possible Jack would encourage crew members to learn swimming, yet still a majority of them did not although *Surprise* probably had more swimmers than most naval ships, and still on nearly every commission Jack has plucked someone from overboard. For his part, Jack was normally a most enthusiastic bather, but less so of late being waterlogged several weeks ago when he dove in behind Stephen who had plunged out a stern window. Now however, with sweltering temperatures, even at night, and the agonizingly languid pace of the ships, Jack had resumed his longtime habit of a dip in the warm sea before breakfast, diving from the leeward cathead and slowly stroking astern along *Surprises*' side to the mizzen chains, it was an exercise Jack relished to a high degree especially the momentary liberation from the onerous responsibilities of a post captain.

Indeed on this morning's swim he was reflecting that they were sailing through an empty glassy sea, where no shipping, fishing, or whaling frequent, with no one to harass them, and none to harass -- that had been the original orders of this mission: to protect British whaling and harass the enemy. Jack dove down, down into the deep green bubbles, with nothing below him for countless fathoms, then lofted to the surface, as the water ran along his naked body and through his long yellow hair; he felt extremely well, and reveled in the present joy of it. He rolled over onto his back and floated, letting his thoughts drift as well, and remembering with a smile that the Admiralty had code-named this mission: 'Project Happiness,' no doubt intending it as an enantiosis, but never to mind, Jack had to admit he was happy enough right now with his course settled for the nonce, however apprehensive he may have been in his own mind regarding the upcoming relations with the Spanish at San Diego.

As each sun drenched day followed upon the other Stephen spent a few more minutes in nude aprication at the foretop cross trees, and each day looked less the pallid Irishman and more the swarthy Catalán, his maternal family. For a tranquil fortnight the earth and sea slowly rotated beneath *Surprise et al.* until she eventually fetched latitude eighteen degrees north and picked up a fresh breeze at last.

Surprise was no longer towing *Enderby*, Bonden and the old *Enderbys* were sailing her, but Jack had left most of the ship's boats still tethered astern of *Enderby*, and he and Bonden had agreed that *Enderby* would sail a more or less direct northerly course while *Surprise* would sail ahead on a broad reach and close tacks, zig-zagging back and forth to search for any shipping and then returning to cross *Enderby* at one hundred and eighteen degrees west longitude, and thus keeping the ships in sight of each other about half the time; or, as Jack described it to Mowett: 'Muchwhat a shepherd dog does in leading sheep, and may we carry a bone in our teeth as well, ha-ha!'

At four bells the breeze began to noticeably stiffen, *Surprises*' new course brought the fresh wind almost upon the frigate's quarter, and Jack called for light hawsers and cablets to the mastheads. 'Mr. Mowett,' he said, 'four good men to the wheel, and let them be relieved at every glass. We are going to crack on.' Topmasts were swayed up, storm-jib, maintopsail and maintopmast staysail, then, for a few minutes, Jack would observe *Surprise* as she took up the heaving thrust of each new sail, gauging her response--a buoyant living response, as they hauled the foresheet aft to tally and belay; and as the strain was increased *Surprise* heeled another strake. 'Mr. Honey,' said Jack, 'pray, have your men line the windward deck,' and the men scrambled up the slanting deck to the weather rail.

White water from the bow wave swept all along the lee side of the ship, flowing in an elegant supine 'S' that washed through the scuppers, and to windward a band of copper could be seen above the streaming waterline as it raced abaft. Jack laid one hand on the hances, feeling the *basso* note of her hull as he might tune his violin, and with his other hand on a backstay appreciating the exact degree of strain. *Surprise* was now really cracking on like smoke and oakum, and it filled Jack with a deep, singular, and familiar boyish pleasure as he gazed ahead through the rigging at the bow surging toward the horizon, and felt the robust speed of the huge living machine beneath him.

This commission had been a reprieve for *Surprise*, she having been slated for a thankless trip to the breaker's yard after her splendid service to two navies going back to the eighties, and her impending doom had become imbued into Jack's thoughts and feelings regarding this entire voyage. While it perhaps might have cast something of a pall across Jack's spirits, instead the bittersweet forestalling of her fate, combined with the now always present realization of her mortality, made this voyage aboard *Surprise* -- made all of Jack's remaining time commanding her -- a precious thing; a very precious thing. And sailing her now, with sundogs jumping in the bowsprit rigging, glissading across the sea with breathtaking celerity, Jack was filled with a feeling of deep aching joy, like a beautiful symphony built from a dense, dissonant chord.

Discreet cheering started forward and spread aft: 'Huzzah! Huzzah! Huzzah!' as Boyle walked cautiously along the sharply sloping deck with the log and reel under his arm, followed by a quartermaster with the sand-glass.

'Double the stray-line,' called Jack.

'Double the stray-line it is, Sir,' replied Boyle, then turned and asked if the glass were clear. He heaved the log and cried: 'Turn!' as the stray-line was away, the sand began to drop, the reel to whir, and the knots to swiftly flit out: eight, ten; every crewman who could spare an eye watched and counted and silently mouthed: 'fourteen, sixteen'...the sand was growing short now as eyes grew wider and darted back and forth from glass to reel. 'Nineteen and a half knots, Sir!' croaked Boyle, with his voice squeaking and cracking and his face looking absolutely astonished. For most it was the fastest speed in memory *Surprise* had ever logged, although Jack knew that probably on at least one occasion he had sailed her a bit faster, but the log-reel was lost overboard.

Jack called to the helmsman: 'Watch your dog-vane,' and then, to Mowett: 'Keep an eye out for patches of cross seas ahead and maintain at least a score and a half of men at the ready to furl the forecourse if need arises.' Jack looked astern at the white water streaming away from the transom, then put his hand back on a mizzen stay and let a satisfying joy wash over him as *Surprise* tantivied along at a wonderfully frightful rate.

Six bells and Mr. Nesbit, panting down the companionway found Doctor Maturin in the orlop deeply engaged in thought, examining a myriad of notes and making some new ones, occasionally referencing one of a half-dozen books strewn on the floor around him. For some time the seed of an idea had been growing in him for a book devoted to the diseases of seamen, and this afternoon he had finally put aside as much time as possible to begin outlining and ordering the proposed chapters such book might contain.

'Beggin' your pardon, Doctor, Sir,' said Nesbit, 'But Captain Aubrey sends his best regards and compliments, and requests your presence at the stern taffrail, and which he said there's not a moment to lose, Sir.'

Stephen looked up from his notes and blinked through his blue spectacles at the cowering Nesbit as if he had just been abruptly awakened from a euphorous dream, and snipped: 'Well then, there's never been a goddamn moment to lose, has there, then? 'Tis only me myself who must lose the moment then, isn't it? To go and see the likes of some flaming sail that scratches the surface of Mercury, or to view the jib-of-jibs, or some other such nonsensicality.'

'But Doctor,' pleaded Nesbit, 'You really must go to a captain when he sends...'

'*Ultima ratio regum*,' said Stephen venomously, and then noticing Nesbit's shock for the first time he said no more, although he inwardly seethed as he climbed the gangway ladder to the top deck while his mind descended down to every dark, contrary, disobliging thing he had ever thought or felt about Jack Aubrey in their long, long friendship.

Stephen had become accustomed to the extreme list of the ship the last hour or so, but now that he was topside it seemed momentarily very disorienting and he had to very carefully work his way aft, to where Jack was leaning back on the rail and smiling, rather stupidly Stephen thought, but he determined to get whatever this was over with, as civilly and quickly as possible, make quick apologies, and return to the orlop post haste.

'You wanted me to see the ship going fast, Jack?' asked Stephen.

'Oh, hello, Stephen,' said Jack, 'What's that? Oh, we've been cracking on like this for some time this afternoon. You don't mean this is the first you've been on deck?' The ship was still logging a wildly exhilarating fifteen knots or so.

'Oh, really, Jack,' said Stephen, 'I must tend my duties, musn't I? I cannot drop everything for every sailor's diversion, now can I?'

Jack was leaning back looking over the rail and grinning: 'I assure you, Stephen, it's no whimsy, I specifically need your expertise and opinion; indeed I dare say you would be the foremost authority one could consult.' Again he smiled and looked over the windward taffrail. 'Is it one of mine, Stephen?'

'One of yours?' Stephen peered over the rail at the water rushing away from the ship, 'What do you mean, Jack?'

'Jack pointed down in the ship's wake, 'There, do you see it? And is it one of mine?'

Stephen peered along the line described by Jack's finger and there it was: a mossy green sea turtle with a rather badly scarred shell was bowling along with *Surprises'* wake at a foudroyant pace. Stephen instantly burst out laughing: 'No, Jack, he's not *aubrea testudo* I'm afraid, not even remotely, though he's the great sea turtle of the world, to be sure, is he not?'

'He certainly is cracking on at an astonishing velocity,' replied Jack, 'we're making over fifteen knots and he's right along with us.'

'Oh, but he's capable of swimming twice again as fast, Jack,' said Stephen, his extreme exasperation of a few seconds ago now given way to extreme excitement as he observed the creature's motions.

'Well,' said Jack, 'I've often seen them in the wake of ships, but not a ship making fifteen knots!'

Stephen was warming to the subject and continued: 'The ship's bottom passing through the water stirs up the many tiny plants and beasties floating near the surface and makes it convenient for the turtle to scoop them up and eat on the run like the Earl of Sandwich, so to say.'

'Plants and animals on the surface did you say?' Jack peered down into the water.

'Oh, yes,' replied Stephen, 'countless myriads of minute animacula, just the sorts of little beasties that clever old cove Leuwenhouk showed to us all, he did.'

'Ah, indeed,' said Jack nodding, 'the surpassing master lens-turner. But still I am quite amazed at a sea turtle flapping along as he is; I had no idea.'

'It makes perfect sense, Jack,' said Stephen, 'for while the ship and the tortoise both share the same favourable current, the tortoise can swim on his own whereas *Surprise* must rely on the wind, or the air if you will. Now, everyone knows that in a race the tortoise will always beat the "air."'

Jack began to laugh so hard tears were forming in his eyes and being swept back his face by the rushing wind, 'Oh, Doctor, aren't you the keen blade today? "The tortoise and the air" is it then? Ha-ha! Stephen, you must tell that one at dinner tonight or I warn you I'll probably make a cock of it trying..."The tortoise and the air,"' he said again, still chortling, 'Capital, just capital.'

'Seeing this old fellow -- ' Stephen leaned over the taffrail and added, 'by the size I conjecture it is a bull -- racing bravely along with us as he is, has a most delightful effect on the spirits this afternoon, does it not , Jack?'

Suddenly Jack looked past Stephen and bawled: 'Belay that, Wilkens!'

Stephen turned and saw Gunner Wilkens lowering a Manton fowling piece whose superbly polished and oiled sight had been trained on the creature.

'But them's fine eating, Captain, Sir, if you please, Sir.' said Wilkens, puzzled.

'Yes, I know,' said Jack somewhat wistfully, 'But not this one. I cannot in good conscience eat any turtle that can outswim *Surprise* when she's logging fifteen knots; even if he ain't one of mine, I'm rather proud of the little fellow.'

'Thank you, Jack,' said Stephen, smiling, 'You may become a natural philosopher after all.'

'I shall accept my chair at the Royal Academy, Doctor, when you are made post.'

The two of them laughed, and so did everyone else within earshot, except Wilkens who was staring forlornly at the turtle still clipping along in a green foaming blur. Stephen also stared at the perfect coordination of the turtle's limbs fustigating through the sea, while the rest of the crew from the foredeck to the quarterdeck all wore a grin. In a mere instant Jack ran his practiced eye across the whole ship from stern to stem, from planksheers to crosstrees, noting the trim, checking the fixed rigging for strain, feeling the rush of wind through his hair off the starboard leech of the mainsail, looking ahead at the run of sea, and far across to where the sea and sky merged in a blue haze. Jack said silently to himself: 'Project Happiness,' as a broad smile spread across his face.

Chapter Four

Enderby sailed the days away, languid and ungainly north, the light winds propelling her in jerks as she rode down the swell and then back up it, her rigging giving a loud clattering groan at the beginning of each descent accompanied far below in the hold by a simultaneous wrenching creak as Jonas worked away at a weak spot in a corner of a bulkhead he'd found in many hours of groping about in the unctuous darkness. The plank appeared to be finally giving way after a great deal of difficult and patient work, such work being necessarily confined to the brief intermittent jounces and bounces of the ship, so as not to be heard by the marine guard just above. Down the ship rode, he waited; up she slid, with a 'crack' almost audible over the clamour of the rigging as she descended again. The plank had not split all the way through, even better it was now sprung sufficiently that Jonas was assured he could squeeze through and let the board spring back in place, making discovery unlikely. Mr. Richards tied a piece of string to a nail head now protruding from the plank, handed the ball of string to Jonas, pulled the plank back and whispered: 'Back before four bells, Davey!' and Jonas slipped through into the utter blackness on the other side. Slowly feeling his way he began carefully exploring the area. Before long his foot kicked something which he picked up and examined by touch and found to be a sailcloth bag with two nails in it. He got down on hands and knees to see if perhaps some of the bag's former contents had spilt out there, but instead his left hand found the sharp end of a broken wine bottle and he could feel wet blood forming, which he wiped on the bag. Putting the bottleneck in the bag he followed the string back to the sprung plank, literally licking his small wound as he went.

'For all the good it does you, Davey,' said Patty Harris quietly as Jonas sat back down, 'just where do you think you'll be goin' out your rabbit hole, Davey?'

'Who knows, Patty?' replied Jonas, 'but listen, Patty:' Jonas spoke very low so the others couldn't hear, 'Our goose is cooked, all us *Hermiones*. Never mind maybe us and a few others had no hand--no hand whatsoever--in all the killings...and never mind that maybe that blackgaurd Captain Pigot deserved killing as well as any man ever did. Either way, to us it don't signify, because unless something drastic is done, we're dished, brother; back in England our lives won't be worth a farthing candle--they'll hang us, Patty, every one of us, sure as you're born.'

'Just as you say,' said Harris, 'but if you escape the hold they'll kill you all the sooner at sea, I should think. We're trapped unless this blubber ferry flounders, in which case we'll no doubt drown.'

'Perhaps,' admitted Jonas, 'but while we're still able I say try to do something, even if it don't answer, as we've naught to lose. I'll go back tomorrow night and reconnoiter a bit more.'

He would go back every night, spending many hours in dispassionate exploration until three bells when he would once again follow the string back to the nail before the marines changed watch at four bells. On the second night his hand touched something hard which proved to be a magnum bottle of port wine. He brought it back and gave it to the others, drinking none himself, but keeping the empty bottle and cork, which he kept hidden behind the plank and gradually filled with water each day from a portion of his personal rations. Mr. Muspratt read for Jonas and some others who did not read, the English label pasted over the bottle's original and declared: 'I must vouchsafe that this is the genuine article, straight from O Porto, Portugal; an excellent choice, Mr. Jonas!'

'I found my thimble-full to have a very upper-class flavour, Lord Davey,' said Richards, adding: 'Tonight, see if you can't find a whole cask of rum, would you now?'

No cask of rum was located that evening or any other, but Jonas did come across a fifteen foot length of hawser, which he could just manage to remove to behind the plank, and then spent hours slowly unraveling it using one of the nails and splicing the whole into a single, staunch, one inch line of almost sixty fathoms length. On subsequent evenings, aside from many rat skeletons, he also came across a hammock-sized piece of oiled tarpaulin with an oilskin cap wrapped inside, a pouch of tobacco (still good), a bag of mostly rotten potatoes, three jars of olives, most of the handle from an apparently broken marlin spike, and a small pile of slate roofing shingles along with a great many empty or not oil casks, and a plethora of odd shaped cargo that threatened to shift and crush him in the dark at any moment. He persisted in this methodical way until one night, a very clear night with a beaming moon, he looked up and spied the moonlight through a crack in the deck above. He spent the rest of that night studying the area and determined that, though now nailed shut, it was in fact a former hatch to the waist of the ship, which in the case of a whaler of *Enderby's* common design, would put him directly above decks, though how far forward or aft he could not tell. At three bells he pushed one of the nails into the crack, tied the string to it, and followed it back to the sprung plank. The following nights he spent all his time trying to gradually push out the nails in the hatch from underneath using a nail for a punch and the marlin spike handle as a hammer.

It was all slow work that provided ample time for reflection, and he was recalling his observations the day he and the others were first put aboard *Enderby*. He had of course, as a sailor, noted her estimated tonnage, keel length and beam breadth, noted how she was laden in the water, how her mizzen was sprung, etc. But now he tried to remember in detail certain areas of the ship; where things were, how gear was stowed, and the *Enderby's* ragabush crew, as well. He remembered some of their faces, and in his mind's eye could still see them now, swinging the lead, lollygagging about the scuttle-butt, rumour-mongering about rebels in Valparaiso and what-not as he and the other *Hermiones* were brought below. He worked away, and he remembered what he could, and he contemplated measures he might contrive to take should his current efforts succeed.

Surprise continued to lask along slightly ahead of *Enderby*, taking in a very large area of sea on long tacks and returning to exchange signals with *Enderby* at least once during daylight hours. Jack had immensely enjoyed this portion of their peregrinations, but in the next day or two *Surprise* would have to return to the mundane escort of *Enderby* as their northerly progress continued, and they began nearing the California coastal waters, notorious for the kind of seas and rolling swells that often sink overladen ships just such as *Enderby*. Nevertheless, for right now Jack stood on the quarterdeck amidst a clear, almost windless, and very starry early evening looking across the whole of the sea. Glowing under the heavens the vast water's surface sparkled and winked all the way out and around the horizon, which appeared somehow even further distant than usual. Jack was trying to locate Jupiter with his night glass when he heard the shout:

'Man overboard!'

The voice shouting Jack recognized immediately as that of Awkward Davis, a clack-handed lob-cock, the very same one whom Jack had once, and then again a second time, to his continued regret, saved from drowning. Jack had had to plunge in to retrieve someone or other on nearly every one of his commissions and he was always somewhat offput accepting the often unduly felicitous, dramatically gratuitous expressions these acts tended to promote in the beneficiary crew members, Awkward Davis' case being the extreme example. Strong as a draught horse, but an able-seaman in name only, he was nonetheless forever after fiercely loyal to Jack to a serious fault, which meant his shipping with Jack whenever possible ever since.

Jack lowered the night glass, looked over the taffrail, and saw the sputtering face slowly going by: it was Davis' recent close companion who'd shipped with him on this commission, Fat-Arse

Jenks, if possible an even greater slubberdegullion than his friend. Plucked as he was from quiet contentment, Jack now found his mind in an unfamiliar state of great and wicked ambivalence, so deep was his wish for someone else to dive in his stead, preferably someone shipping off *Surprise* before the next commission. When no such person was forthcoming, he finally gave the order to sheet the forecourse and bring the helm up, telling two quartermasters to find an empty water cask and tie a length of cablet around it. He then removed his shoes, coat, and breeches, told the quartermasters to put the empty puncheon over the side and to keep their eyes clapped on him as he dove over the hanses, swam to the keg and, grasping the cablet, swam with it over to the terrified Jenks who, for all his thrashing about, seemed to be remaining afloat above the water's surface, not sinking like a stone as Doctor Maturin so often did on his frequent errant dippings. When Jenks finally recognized his rescuer he tried to regain some composure and soon he was holding to the barrel while Jack slowly swam toward *Surprise*, a rich effluvium of phosphorescent sparks surrounding them and trailing them the whole of the way back to the ship.

The following evening as he and Stephen applied themselves to a somewhat difficult Haydn duet, it suddenly occurred to Jack that he never did gain a sighting of Jupiter, and he resolved to do so tomorrow if the clear weather held. At that moment, Stephen's 'cello concluded a phrase and he insensibly improvised a very graceful ending turn, taking the perfect fourth to a minor seventh, providing a lovely context for Jack's violin to enter with a bold stabbing attack on the D major tonic, as Stephen now slowly bowed back and forth the reinforcing roots to Jack's arpeggios. As Stephen had hoped, of late he and Jack had had opportunity to play virtually every night and especially Stephen's playing, but also Jack's had noticeably benefited from the regular practise. Both were passably competent amateur musicians, with Jack perhaps the more adept by nature, and both had a deep abiding appreciation of music. But for the nonce circumstances had allowed them the rare opportunity to sharpen their skills to an exceptional focus, and latterly their musical improvisations were often an intoxicating inspiration to both, albeit still with an occasional small gaffe. It was so improved, in fact, that even Killick now sometimes sat just outside the door of the great cabin, secretly listening to it, latently rejoicing in it.

That night as Stephen lay sleeping in his berth he dreamt of 'cello; indeed, he bowed his way completely through all four parts of Mozart's *Quartet in F Major*. But as he played his vivid recollection of the piece began to fade and it was replaced by a quiet staccato rhythm that grew more and more dense and insistent, reaching a crescendo with a loud knock on the cabin door which woke him abruptly.

'Doctor Maturin, kind gentleman, all praise to Saint Patrick be with you, Sir.'

Stephen rubbed his eyes and blinked, 'What is it, then, Padeen, and the dear be with you,' and noticed he could still hear a dull, but very dense with many beats, drumming sound.

'Begging pardon,' said Padeen in English, 'Mr. Maitland sends his compliments and ask you topside at your very first convenience, he said you'd wish to be woke for to see them, sir... very pretty bird fish...'

When Stephen arrived on deck Jack and Mowett had already joined Maitland under the moonlight to view an outlandish spectacle as an enormous school of small, shiny, flying fish about two feet in length, with enlarged, diaphanous pectoral fins for 'wings' filled all the sea and air about them to a height of about twenty feet like a swarm of locusts. Scores of them were landing aboard, and men were gathering them up in buckets. Stephen had heard sailors speak of such swarms, but had hitherto dismissed them as just the sort of apocryphal yarn sailors spin when practising upon the gullible.

'Isn't it quite amazing, Doctor?' asked Jack.

'I wouldn't have believed it,' said Stephen, 'They are, I believe, ordinary *Dactylopterus*, flying fish, as we have seen before this, but never such a profuse and frightening bounty of them.'

'Now that we're in California waters, we may see the likes of it again,' said Jack as the school passed at last, leaving hundreds of their numbers behind on deck.

'That was the strange sight of the world to be sure,' said Stephen, as dozens flopped all around them and men gathered them up, 'Pray, how are they for eating then, Jack?'

'Well, actually they're rather bony and mean,' replied Jack, 'but they are a matchless bait for bonito, and *they* are quite gustable, I assure you, fresh or salted; meat as white and flaky as one of Sophie's pie crusts, and I'm sure with a squall of flying fish the size of the one just past that a horde of Spanish mackerel, as they used to call them, won't be far behind. In a few days we re-group with *Enderby* and if we're lucky anglers we can feed *Surprise* and fill all the prisoner's belly's with a jolly good treat as well.'

By two bells that very evening Jonas had at last removed the final nail sealing the waist hatch. After waiting and listening for some minutes he slowly lifted the hatch about four inches wide at what he took to be its' starboard side and took a furtive peek which confirmed his bearings. He was in the aft waist, not far from the starboard mizzen chains. Near the rail in the bleached moonlight he even captured a glimpse of half a dozen casks, still standing in their places on the deck as he remembered them, hard by the mizzen chains. He quietly lowered the hatch back down and rove the two nails at opposite corners from underneath, to keep it from moving underfoot. Then he followed the string back to the space behind the plank where he had hidden the magnum bottle (now full of water), the sixty fathom line, and a number of the other items discovered in his explorations of the hold.

Patty Harris, the only *Hermione* actually privy to details of Jonas' plan, wished him luck along with the others, and taking a number of the found items with him Jonas followed the string back to the hatch, as the moon and stars moved in and out from behind the amassing cloud cover. At the sound of three bells he took a quick look fore and aft out the hatch and saw no one. Moving with silent, willful precision, he slid it open and placed the rope, the sailcloth bag, and the bottle up on deck. He took a glance each way and then deftly sprung up through the hatch and lay very still a moment. His heart was beating very fast and very loudly in his chest, but to his great relief no one heard except he.

Presently the thickening umber coloured cumulus draped both the sea and sky in deep blackness and looking aft the only light Jonas could now see was the dim xanthic glow of the binnacle lamp. He could see the silhouette of the master against it, checking the course and apparently facing the opposite direction. Noiselessly Jonas slipped over the starboard rail, worked his way aft to the mizzen chains, took the sailcloth bag containing the few good potatoes, the olives, and the piece of tarpaulin, and slid it through the rail behind the casks. Seeing that two of the barrels near the rail were empty, he tightly secreted the bag on the deck between them, then climbed down into the plates bringing the bottle and the rope. He bent one end of the line to the underside of a lower shroud, and the other around the neck of the bottle, and slowly lowered it into the water. The mate of the watch came aft briefly carrying a spirit lamp, and Jonas clung stock-still against *Enderby's* hull like a barnacle. But when the mate returned forward it gave Jonas an excellent brief view of the deck and rigging. When he was left in blackness again he began working his way forward along the outside of the rail until he reached the main chains, where he rested very mute, listening for any sound aside from his own heart.

The deck was deserted as ever it could be, notwithstanding, there were still many men aboard this vessel between the original *Enderbys*, the *Norfolks*, and the marine guards, and Bonden and the number of other *Surprises*. British all, except the *Norfolks*, and the *Norfolks* are Americans after all, now sailing as prisoners of war, and they no longer held any deference for the *Hermiones* whatsoever; so to be detected by anyone would be fatal. His arms were already starting to ache severely from the long stealthy obreption to the main chains, and this was only the beginning. For the first time since he'd sprung the plank in that weakened section of bulkhead he felt fear of his escape. At the outset he'd known that failure was a likelihood, but now that looming probability seemed dreadfully clearly drawn. There were so many things aside from brute physical strength, so many tenuous and untenable things, that he would be sorely depending on now, nor was fool's luck the least of them. Saying he would hang in any event were he not to escape is all well and large when one is merely planning to escape, hoping to escape; but the devil is in the doing of the escape.

The mate came round with his lamp again and when he'd gone forward Jonas ducked down low and followed him, quickly moving along the outside of the rail, sychronizing his handfalls with the mate's footsteps, until he reached the forechains, and there waited again to observe the situation. It was just before first light and the clouds appeared to be lowering. The wind had fallen to a puff, and though the forecourse was set, he could not see a soul anywhere in the foremast rigging. As four bells was sounded he seized on the diversion to quickly climb the futtocks to the topyard, and there lay flat across the yard so as not to be seen, at least not yet.

The changing marine guards in the hold were each completing their third head count, and impossible though it may seem, they were a man short. Word was sent to wake Bonden who immediately called for tripling the guard, while two men with lamps searched the onboard gaol for a possible hidey-hole, finding instead an escape route to a dauntingly capacious hiding place, even to those with lamps to guide them.

With the sun half risen Jonas observed the change of watch below on deck. He recognized the lone marine on deck as Westerdale, and he presumed all the other marines were probably engaged in the search for him below. But many of the *Enderbys*, including Tanzi Jones and Nic Crofter, were now swarming on deck, casting long shadows to westward, toward the larboard side, in the amber early dawnlight. Conditions were perfect, and Jonas, having regained his usual feckless sangfroid, stood up and balanced on the larboard topyard.

A moment later a broken marlin spike handle clattered through the foremast halyards, nearly striking Nic, and causing half the watch to look up to the foretop where Jonas was spotted immediately. Westerdale turned, saw Jonas in the shadowy morning light, brought his musket up to his cheek, and demanded in a loud voice that Jonas promptly climb down to be put in chains the rest of the voyage. Tanzi was coming towards him through the starboard futtocks and would soon be aloft. Jonas took three small steps to larboard, to the very tip of the yard, and sprung from it toward the water. Westerdale fired, Jonas' left hand went to his gut and blood was seen to gush by several crewmen as he fell down, down and down through the air and, splashing into the water, sank out of sight in the deep with the whole of the watch agape over the larboard rail in astonishment.

As Jack had privately suspected, *Surprise* had gained further offing from *Enderby* than was intended and she was not seen until late forenoon two days later at which time Jack gave the order to turn helm up and approach. By the time noon readings had been taken the ships were close enough to exchange signals. Jack watched the quarterdeck of *Enderby*, where he could make out the gold earrings, the large, strong-built frame, and the long pigtail of Barrett Bonden, looking very officious and commanding indeed as he gave his orders to the signal lieutenant; The whole effect of the scene caused Jack to smile as he observed through his glass. He knew Bonden was loathe to spell out any signal not already in the vocabulary, and Jack had come to relish the cryptic ambiguity of some recent communiqués as another of the particular and enjoyable aspects of this on-the-whole very pleasant, if just a bit errant, cruise. This time, however, the signal was distinct-- and not at all pleasant:

'One Prisoner Dead'

When *Surprise* had drawn to within half a cable length she hove to, and Mr. Butcher came to the rail with a speaking trumpet asking if Doctor Maturin could lend assistance with Captain Palmer, whose already grave condition had precipitately worsened. Jack, who required no speaking trumpet to be clearly heard, preferred Doctor Maturin to stay aboard *Surprise*; Mr. Butcher replied that Palmer could not possibly be moved. Finally, Stephen arrived on deck.

'Shall the whole of the world share in the medical facts of Captain Palmer's case, then? Or shall we shout them across the seven seas, our patient's complaints and symptoms? And then we'll have the surgeon halloo back with his diagnosis and prescriptive advice, will we, Jack?'

Stephen looked across at Butcher, who was now anxiously waiting at the rail.

'Pray, Jack, send me over with Mowett in one of the boats and I'll do what I can and return within three hours.'

'Well...' Jack rubbed his chin, 'I'd like to get a first hand account of this dead prisoner myself...'

Stephen was silent but looked questioningly at Jack, who continued:

'I don't know any of the medical particulars, Doctor, nor any of the particulars at all, for all that. Bonden merely signaled that a prisoner had died aboard Enderby, and I call that reason enough to grant your request of a boat, so allow me to offer you my boat with my compliments, and I'll go along with you myself.'

The boat was put out and Jack, Mowett, a couple of mids, Padeen, and lastly Stephen were all landed safely; safety being an uppermost concern in the case of Doctor Maturin, his numerous mishaps regarding bosun's chairs and boarding planks being well known amongst *Surprises*, and they being uncommonly fond of their Ship's Surgeon.

In a few minutes pulling on the sweeps they reached *Enderby*, where painstaking care was again taken in bringing Stephen on board without mishap. Stephen and Mister Butcher repaired to the cockpit to tend Captain Palmer, while Jack and Bonden met in *Enderby's* after cabin.

'Well,' said Jack upon speaking with Bonden, 'I expected it would be a *Hermione*, poor devil. So they shot him right off the foretop yard, then?'

'Oh, yes sir, Captain,' said Bonden, 'the whole morning watch saw it with me. He was mortally wounded and he knew it: tried executed and buried at sea, all of a single stroke, as you might say, Sir. He was a fool in the first instance to climb into the foretop rigging, Sir, that was his undoing; that and this marine marksman Westerdale.'

'Yes, very good musket practise, wasn't it?' and Jack added candidly, 'Who is to say he ain't better off than those mates he left behind, Mister Bonden? But what is the case as you see it with the remaining *Hermiones*?'

'Well, Sir,' said Bonden, 'none of the others tried to escape that we know of. Which they was all there at the start of the head count, excepting this one, this fellow David Jonas. When I went back down to the hold, and they learned what had become of their mate, in the main they took it very hard, Sir.'

'Are you expecting any further trouble then?' asked Jack.

'Oh, I shouldn't think so, Sir, no,' said Bonden. 'Their factotum, as it were, a Mister Muspratt by name, inquired as to the disposal of the remains, and requested a memorial services. But when they learnt he'd been shot and lost overboard, and so we hadn't no remains to memorialize; well, they got quite upset, Sir, quite upset, indeed. Which, it seems this Jonas was a popular mate and known to be an intrepid soul, and this escape of his had got up foolish hopes and what not amongst themselves.'

'Well, that is where they can have their bloody memorial,' said Jack, 'amongst themselves. I'll not have them out of confinement, and the last thing I need is a service for this prisoner above board on deck. I'll see if I can persuade Reverend Martin to be pulled over by someone.'

In *Enderby's* cockpit, Stephen motioned Mister Butcher, who did not have Latin, out of the hearing range of Captain Palmer and whispered: 'It is a remarkable state of decrepity, advanced by half again since last I observed him. He now displays some of the marthamble-like neuropathetical discomfitures: the sunken eyes, limbs withered, loss of acuity, breath foul...'

'Would it do to bleed him then, Doctor?' asked Mister Butcher.

'I shouldn't think so, no,' said Stephen, 'not in this latitude, but I think getting him up on deck in clear weather might answer nobly. It would appear his suffering is due to quartan ague and melancholia, much exacerbated by the exigent antecedent factors inherent aboard a ship at sea. I should like to get some sassafras bark and jesuits root at the first opportunity.'

'Well I, for one,' said Butcher, 'hope to get some decent tobacco at the next opportunity. Some time ago I dropped my pouch someplace on *Enderby*, with all my best tobacco in it.'

'That really is rather dreadful,' said Stephen, who still felt the sting from an instance in which the ship's rats found and devoured all his carefully stowed Brasilian coca leaves.

Some relief for Mister Butcher was on its' way in the form of three cigars in the abstemious Martin's pocket, two of which he would eventually part with upon hearing Butcher's sad tale. Martin had concealed his bible under his coat, but every one knew the true nature of his visit was in his capacity as a parson, and not as a ships surgeon's assistant, and thus it was perhaps going to be very bad luck.

They all watched quietly as he was raised up in the bosun's chair and brought aboard *Enderby*. The unspoken consensus was clear; let him perform his duties privately and quickly, in a seamanlike fashion, and then perhaps there would be no real trouble.

The day was grey and overcast with a small choppy sea, and between the poor visibility, all the speculation and anxiety about luck and ill omens, and the constant activity of boats ferrying between ships with important shipboard personages, no one noticed the solitary bather under a grey oilskin cap, who had been slowly, silently swimming all the while toward *Surprise* from sixty fathoms astern of *Enderby*. When he had reached *Surprises*' stern he hid himself on the starboard side of the rudder, kept the cap well down over his face and rested against the transom. After some minutes he peeked about him and determined that no one could see him here, nor were they looking for him. Taking great care not to touch the rudder itself, thus alerting the man at the wheel something was amiss, he contrived to climb up the stern using two hands and a foot on the keel, while the other foot advanced up the strakes. At first this proved efficient enough, then an old grape wound reasserted itself in his keel foot with a deep cutting pain that made him feel suddenly weak to his core.

By now in his advance up the stern he was suspended almost horizontally from the outward slope of *Surprises*' transom. To fall now with a splash would be disastrous, and so he bolstered his resolve enough to bring both feet up to perch on the top gudgeon. He looked up and thanked fortune when he noticed for the first time the bars protruding near the stern window bottoms.

Jack had had these bars shipped some months back as a safety precaution after Stephen fell overboard through one of the stern ports earlier in this voyage. That misadventure had found Stephen and Jack apparently 'saved' by a small, most unusual appearing group of south sea-faring women, who handled their exotic fore-and-aft rigged craft--a catamaran affair consisting of a canoe and out-rigger with a cabin deck athwart ships, and called a *tuamotu pahi*--with astonishing skill and implausibly close to the wind. As events later proved, Jack and Stephen were more captured than saved actually, and these women intended to unsex them. Stephen was barely able to effect their escape by pointing to Jack's groin at a propitious moment and repeating loudly several times: '*Taboo*!' the only Polynesian word that the polyglot philologist Doctor Maturin could think of. When they were both back aboard *Surprise*, suitably chastened, as it were, Jack added these safety bars at the window bottom to ally any future, similar occurrences.

They now proved serviceable handles for Jonas to clap on to, as his feet and knees shinnied the strakes on the transom. He sorely desired to rest his arms at this juncture, but this posture offered no prospect of that. He briefly glanced to larboard and saw with shock how utterly visible he was at this moment, should anyone care to look his way.

With a hope that no one would, he hauled himself up and through the open stern window in a single motion, falling into the great cabin and bumping the 'cello which fell with a low, ringing thud against Stephen's music stand, the curious cabinet that Dianna Villiers had gifted him years ago. Jonas sprung to his feet, took a quick look about the cabin, darted beneath the large desk and hid, and not a moment too soon.

The door from the coach cabin opened and Killick came in to investigate the noise. He put the 'cello back where the Doctor had placed it against the window ledge and then noticed water on the deck under the 'cello, where he had just swabbed this morning. It not only puzzled Killick that he missed this spot, it worried him that perhaps the 'cello fell on his account.

'Toil and moil, toil and moil,' lamented Killick, who went back to the coach to retrieve a swab.

Jonas was on hands and knees in the footwell of the great desk, as compact as ever he could make himself. His left foot still seared with pain, while all his limbs ached as never they had before, and now some irregularity in the sole of the deck was pressing hard against his right knee. Before he could determine what it was or even shift his position, Killick returned, still muttering sundry imprecations as he dried up the water, while a few feet away Jonas silently prayed his own adjurations; prayers that he did not leave a trail of droplets straight to his hiding place.

When Killick resumed work in the coach, Jonas tried to make

his right knee comfortable and found that a board in the deck was loose and a corner was prodding into his knee. He pivoted the board up and found a hidden compartment with a thin metal box in it. He put the board back down and waited some long minutes in silence to assure no one else was coming. Waited, and while he waited he wondered; what could be in it?

He knew that officers on board ships often kept hidden certain personal items of jewelry; watches, medals, and the like, in the belief, or hope, that even if they are taken, the enemy may never find it before being retaken, at which time they may retrieve their belongings undisturbed.

He reasoned that it was most likely some important sorts of ship's papers: signal codes, admiralty orders and the like. If they were, he thought, they could prove useful if he survived to get ashore at Valparaiso. If rumours were true, and the rebels had taken the port, perhaps he could parlay his situation ashore, and convince the rebels to attack *Enderby* and free his mates. Then he wondered if they all might welcome his help; there were, he thought, among the *Hermiones*, at least one or two less daring that would rather go before the Admiralty's court martial and hang under the law as a mutineer, than become a traitor to Britain and the King. But he knew that for himself and most of the others at this point it would be far better to take their chances with all the barbarous rebels of South America than to hang at home as Englishmen.

Several more minutes of like ruminations; long moments of solitude, and Jonas ventured to remove the box and more closely examine it. It was locked and sealed, but not very securely, somewhat attenuating hopes. He broke the wax seal and pried the clasp open without making too much noise: the contents proved to be some very official looking papers of a type Jonas had never before seen. It certainly wasn't a code book, he had seen those before this, and it didn't have any latitudes or longitudes as orders would, and there were no charts in the box. It looked more to Jonas like deeds of some sort, or maybe insurance papers, covered with official seals and signatures and with many numbers on it. He hadn't expected anything like these papers, and he really hadn't time for conjecture, so he scooped up the lot of them and put them under his shirt. He closed the box, put it back in its' cubby, and put the sprung butt back in place on top.

He got out from beneath the desk and went to the companionway door to listen. There was no marine sentry posted since Captain Aubrey was currently aboard *Enderby*, so Jonas merely walked into the companionway and out to the starboard gun deck near the mizzen chains. Everyone on deck was either aloft or at the larboard rail looking towards *Enderby*, so he slipped over the rail to hide momentarily in *Surprises*' starboard mizzen chains, thinking to himself that it was becoming quite a habit with him now.

For the last two days he'd survived his ordeal of being towed behind *Enderby* by pulling his way hand over hand back to the starboard chains at two bells in the evening watch, wrapping up in the patch of tarpaulin and sleeping until an hour or so before first light. He would then awaken, have some olives and potato for breakfast, then stow everything, grab his sixty fathom line, get back into the briny sea and go to the end of his rope, the irony of which was not lost on him. There he had the magnum of fresh water to wash it all down. He had planned carefully up to that point and it had answered miraculously; now he would have to contrive as he went.

He jumped back over the rail and crept into the jolly boat. There he hid under a pair of sails and waited for nightfall to determine his next move. He fell asleep immediately, deeply, and for many hours, undetected and undisturbed.

He woke parched with thirst, and from under the sailcloth could tell it was in the fullness of day. He could hear sea birds squeaking their rusty hinges flying above the ship, and he could smell land. Enough sunlight penetrated through the sailcloth for Jonas to see the bilge of the jolly boat, where the water appeared relatively clean, and Jonas reasoned that it must be mostly rain water left over from all the recent drenchings; thus convinced it wasn't really bilge water, he drank gratefully.

He then lay there a long time considering his thorny predicament. Once they were in port he would surely be discovered, which meant there was little time. Despite the fact that no one was really looking for him, the sole factor in his favour, even by his own accounting, nonetheless he would certainly be found when the bum boats brought lady visitors out for the sailors. Indeed, this jolly boat was an ideal setting for such a rencontre, and for that matter, at any moment now it was wholly possible the Captain of *Surprise* himself could desire to use this very jolly boat for any number of non-carnal purposes.

He decided his only option was to wait out in this position up until *Surprise* made port and try to slip out unnoticed as another of the sailors. He still had ten shillings Pat Harris had given him the night he escaped, and surely any bum boat master would ferry him ashore for two.

He now turned his attention to making himself as presentable and inconspicuous as possible. Though his shirt was badly torn, sea water had removed any blood stain caused when Jonas had superficially cut his own torso with the broken bottle neck. It had been a shockingly effective ruse, but so many subsequent hours soaking in salt water had kept the cut from healing, and now that he had thoroughly dried out, each of the cuts had formed deep, calloused cracks that would open and bleed at the slightest suggestion. He still had his cravat in his pocket, so he took it out and fashioned a bandage from it. His lack of shoes presented no problem, since most sailors would naturally be barefoot in this latitude anyway. His breeches would not well bear the meanest scrutiny, but they were in one piece and kept him covered as a proper Christian, so they would have to do. He determined to get as much sleep as possible before he attempted this most hazardous next ambit, since by his guess they would probably make port at Valparaiso within a day or so.

His accounting of the time in this instance was about right, but his judgement of location was in error by some fifty-five hundred leagues.

Chapter Five

The breeze fell to nothing in the middle watch and both ships hove to under fore courses and close-reefed topsails. The calm continued into the foggy morning hours until almost six bells in the forenoon watch when a stiff onshore wind blew the clouds off, and although there was no apparent swell, there were small horses in the short seas all around. It blew from about three points forward of the larboard beam, and though she griped a bit in the chop *Surprise* logged a brisk nine knots at noon, when readings showed her position at thirty-two degrees and forty minutes of latitude North. At five past noon Calumny called out from the maintop that he could see land six points off the starboard bow to the north by northeast, and by a quarter past all on deck could see the low headland covered with what looked like a sparse topping of scrub trees and brush.

Captain Aubrey and First Mate Mowett were observing from the starboard mizzen taffrail, and as they approached closer and closer, and finally rounded the point Jack looked through the glass and said:

'Yes, that would be Ballast Point. and there's the beautiful large bay beyond it, just as Van Couver's drawings have it; a very snug little harbor, and as smooth as a duck pond.'

Mowett's cheerful gaze went out past the bay to the high cliffs that fronted a long chain of hills, going back as far as the eye could see; his first glimpse of a mainland in many trying months. 'Is there not a Spanish village at this bay, Captain?' he asked.

'Well,' said Jack, 'I assume it's in the nature of a village, although they are rightly called "missions," of course. I do know that the last few years there's been a going trade in furs and hides, mostly to China of all places, but I take it there are still less than a thousand of Christians, not counting the Indian converts, you understand. There are a great many Indians and a very few friars; their fortress, or "presidio," as they call it, houses perhaps a few score of men, I suppose, and then there are Spanish government officials and their families, and no doubt at least a few families of settlers; merchants, dockside workers, and the like. But I see little evidence thus far of anything."

Jack looked over his left shoulder and saw Doctor Maturin approaching. 'Ah, Stephen, how very happy I am to see you. You see I've delivered your California after all.'

'Are you quite sure, Jack?' asked Stephen, 'It's a rather barren looking place to be California, is it not, my dear? Although,' he went on without awaiting a reply, 'to be sure some places appear mean at first, and later prove to be deliciously rich in some other way, as the season we spent on Desolation Island. Pray, may I use your glass?'

Stephen peered through the lens and swept his eye along the empty beach. At last by the bay he spotted two large, rough-hewn boarded buildings that resembled nothing so much as the ice houses erected on Newcastle River in the winter. Some movement caught the corner of Stephen's eye and he swung the glass southward and aimed it at a most extraordinary sight: at first it appeared like a waterfall or a landslide, but with beautiful streams of colour woven all through it, and even mixing all about in it, as the whole amorphous mass descended the hillside in a blurred design. Suddenly Stephen recognized with a smile that the animated specks of colour were in fact dogs--scores and scores of dogs and their offspring who had been left off or lost here by passing ships. Stephen tried to estimate their numbers, but could only conclude it was a few hundreds of dogs, dogs of every size shape and breed. Not the sort of exotic fauna Stephen had hoped for, but it was a start.

With *Enderby* still some distance astern, *Surprise* hove to just outside the narrow harbor entrance in the lee of the point, and Jack ordered the King's colours sent aloft and a single gun to be fired to windward. After some minutes a bell rang back in response, and Jack could see there was a ferry or small, barge-like craft, about twenty-five feet long with a very shallow draft, coming through the channel and towards *Surprise*. It was the *Fernbrook*, a disembarcadero shuttle, carrying its' pilot and two Franciscan monks. One priest was an open-faced obsequious novice, perhaps a clerk for the elder padre, a stern looking man of about forty with dark, deep-set eyes on a very tanned face, who sat bolt upright in the bow with one hand clenched tightly on the starboard gunnel, looking straight at Jack. Jack was just about to raise his arm and call out a greeting when the monk bolted up from his seat.

'Father, *por favor*!' shouted the pilot, '*Cuidado*, be careful, or you'll take a swim!'

Ignoring him, the monk cupped his hands to his mouth and shouted: '*Señor*! *Ingles marinaros*! I am sorry! You may not enter the bay, and the ship's company is not allowed ashore here!'

'The devil you say,' said Jack quietly, smiling and waving back.

The three were brought aboard amid the customary military etiquette and politely escorted to the quarterdeck by a very chipper Mowett, somewhat softening Friar De La Valle's mood.

'Right this way, Padre, there you are,' said Mowett as he led the trio past the marine sentry and into the great cabin. De La Valle removed his broad-brimmed hat and bent under the beam as he entered. There, in addition to Jack, were Jack's acting clerk, Mr. Blackeney, and Stephen, ostensibly to assist in translating, although De La Valle proved to have an excellent command of English. But Stephen was Roman Catholic, like these men, and Jack felt more comfortable having him present, in case the situation called for some of Stephen's particular finesse.

The situation would. After some lengthy introductions it

was learned that the novice's name was Jean-Pedro Baptiste, whom had been ordained in Seville two years previous, and having been here in San Diego for about a year spoke only Spanish, and appeared to Stephen quite ready to return to Seville at the first affordable opportunity. The pilot of the *Fernbrook*, Jack Ditler, on the other hand, spoke the local colloquial English well, and quite readily. Some years ago he had been aboard a Boston trading vessel in port here that sailed without him and then sank not a week later near Point Concepcione and he became a permanent resident.

Jack assured Friar De La Valle that his was a moral and upright Christian King's ship. That he, Jack Aubrey, did not, for example, tolerate the practice of allowing bumboats bringing whores out to his ship to corrupt both man and boy aboard, and that his was a ship with a parson (forgetting for the moment that he kept him listed as a surgeon's assistant to avoid the bad luck of a parson aboard), where church was rigged each Sunday without fail, and the Articles of War read to the men.

'Capitan Aubrey,' began De La Valle, 'this is all to the good, I'm sure, but you see, the last English ship here stole some of the hides, even though they had been told not to do so. It is for this reason we can only allow your ships to be within one league of shore.'

'Oh, is that all?' smiled Jack, 'Why we've no intentions at all regarding any hides, I assure you, Padre. My intentions are merely to procure some certain small stores, such as tobacco and sugar, and to re-fill our drinking water casks. Of course, my men would all like very much to go ashore as well, as we have all been these last many weeks at sea. I expect that it will be to both our mutual benefit, do you not, Padre?'

De La Valle, who had had his head slightly tilted to his left, now shifted subtly to the right. 'No. You see, Capitan, I respect your words, and I wish to believe you are the honourable man you certainly appear to be,' his head shifted back left again, 'we are labouring for the last several years but have yet to complete an aqueduct from the east. Water is very precious here, you see?' He was tilted decidedly left now, 'and ours is a very poor mission, we cannot have all the men from two mighty vessels such as yours,

Capitan Aubrey, running over all the countryside. We can allow you what water as you may find at Whaler's Spring south of Ballast Point, but you shall have to ferry it to your ships a league away. We cannot let anyone ashore.

'No, Capitan, I can see no other way that would not be very bad for us, I fear. I trust you will honour my wishes, Capitan Aubrey.'

Jack was momentarily non-plussed, but still barely holding the corners of his mouth up, Jean-Pedro was staring out to sea through the stern windows longingly, and finally Jack Ditler knitted his eyebrows and broke the silence:

'Padre, *por favor*, but if we don't let anybody ashore, I shant be able to afford my regular donation to the mission on Sundays--toward the building of the church.'

'Perhaps, Padre,' said Jack, 'I could arrange to loan some of my men to assist you with this church building--or the aqueduct--while we're here. Surely we can let some ashore, can we not? I only expect to be here about ten days, weather and tide permitting.'

De La Valle was still tilting left, however tempting this offer may have been. 'No...I don't see how...I cannot change the rules.'

Stephen turned to De La Valle and said in Spanish: 'Might it be possible for myself and some other Catholics aboard to come ashore to hear mass and give confession, Padre? It would mean a great deal to the men and myself to receive communion, and I wish to make a donation toward the church building as well.'

'You are a Catholic, Doctor? I did not expect such a thing on an English ship.' He thought silently for a moment then turned to Jack distinctly tilting right again and said in English: 'Capitan Aubrey, I see you are a man of honour after all. And we are a poor but honourable mission.' The corners of Jack's mouth were slowly becoming weightless again, 'Perhaps I could discuss your case with the Commandant at the Presidio, along with some certain provisos, some very strict rules upon which I must insist, and we may be able to accommodate each other.'

Father De La Valle paused for a moment and no one in the room spoke. Jack was genuinely smiling now, but deliberately holding his tongue for once.

De La Valle's head now tilted to neither side, but was straight up and down, and he said: 'I will take yourself, Capitan, Doctor Maturin and the other Catholics ashore with us right now, if you wish. There is a chapel inside the Presidio near the Commandant's office where I can provide the sacraments to the men.

'I trust, Capitan Aubrey, that you will vouch for the honour of any of those who may be allowed ashore. They are not to overrun our gardens, or harass or molest my children, that is, the Indians, in any way. Especially the women. And I would ask you not provide spirits or otherwise try to corrupt the Indians, and this I say for all of them, both my children and the gentiles, those Indians who are not yet baptized in the Holy Lord.

'As far as water goes, I am afraid in all cases you will have to work very hard to obtain the great deal of water you must need for your ships. Often water is only where one can find it this season of the year.'

'Understood,' said Jack, 'and if any man is found guilty of any unChristianlike behaviour towards you or your Indians, Padre, I shall personally see to it they are flogged, you have my word. If possible, I should like to get ashore then as quickly as possible, as there's not a moment to lose before nightfall.'

'Excellent.' Father De La Valle stood up, greatly startling Jack Ditler, who had been staring out the stern windows along with Jean-Pedro, but rather than daydreams of Seville, he had been estimating the extent of his possible windfall should things go as smoothly at the Presidio.

His first fare ashore proved worrisome, however, as aside from the Jacks (Aubrey and Ditler) both large men themselves, among the Catholics was not only the lumbering Padeen but the elephantine Fat-Arse Jenks who was made to sit nearly dead-center amid-ship down low between the thwarts of the *Fernbrook* to keep the shallow fore-and-aft rigged craft from swamping.

On the beach by the wooden buildings were now gathered a score of men, most in red shirts and large straw hats, several were on fast horses riding up and down the beach with a brace of barking dogs in chase behind them, hallooing to their friends in a most outrageous fashion, occasionally performing tricks of horse handling.

'Pray, who are those horsemen, and what are those buildings behind them?' asked Stephen.

'Them's Sandwich Islanders,' said Jack Ditler, adopting the tone of a cicerone 'and they're done working today, so they celebrate. They work the hide houses, those funny looking buildings, and they drough hides when the big shippers come in. Sandwich Islanders are real good seamen, too, Sir, to a man they are, Sir.' Ditler looked at Stephen but couldn't see his eyes through the blue spectacles, 'They generally move about 'twixt here and home, and some also spend time in South American waters; Peru and Chilé mostly. They're up and down the Pacific, but few will go 'round the horn, as they can't stand to the cold so well.'

'They're superb horsemen are they not?'

'Oh, yeah, but they're just showing away; it's their way of greeting you I suppose. They're right friendly people, the Sandwich Islanders are; and I can tell you they will give you their last *real* if you're a friend, their *aikáne* as they call them. And they're most all Christians, the ones crewing on ships and moving about the world sea, that is. They wouldn't be of the kind that ate poor old Captain Cook...'

'And that was over thirty years ago, was it not?' asked Stephen.

'That's right. My, my, how fast this world changes, does it not, Doctor?'

'And how rarely for the better? But look, the sun is coming out.' Indeed, after a gloomy morning it was turning into a most beautiful day.

On shore an Indian holding two horses awaited De La Valle, and reported that another Indian had gone in search of more horses.

'Where will he get them?' asked Jack, turning to Stephen who asked in Spanish.

'*¿Quien sabe?*' shrugged the Indian, and so they waited.

After a few minutes two of the Sandwich Islanders, followed by a small pack of dogs, came riding up from the direction of the hide houses on magnificent looking horses. They rode bareback, grasping the mane, no shoes on either horse or rider. They both wore red sailors shirts, but the taller of the two was also wearing a sort of kilt garment made of a jute-like fabric and dyed in bright colours. He was otherwise soundly built, with a square-cut chin and a broad frame, dark brown eyes and copper-skin, but improbably redheaded, having it in short curls that fell round his ears and freckled cheeks. The other was stouter, with a large, round friendly face and shining dark eyes framed by very thick, very straight, very dark hair, which he wore braided in the back, not in the old-fashioned navy way, but in two braids, one on either side.

The redhead smiled, revealing large white teeth and said in remarkably clear English:

'*Aroha kákou!* Hello Father De La Valle. Do your English friends need horses?'

'Yes, but where has become of that boy, the one they all call Luis Loco, who used to catch the horses for us?'

'He's been gone all day. Some of my *kanakas* tell me they saw him talking to a sailor from one of your ships,' he nodded toward Jack and the rest of the *Surprises*, 'who came ashore just about noon.'

'We're the only ones to disembark thus far,' said Jack, and the others all nodded.

'Well, no matter, I know where he keeps his saddles, so we two *kanakas* will fetch horses for you, no charge today, Father! Ha-ha-ha!' He looked to his companion and they both laughed heartily as they rode off in two different directions.

Jack Ditler volunteered the Sandwich Islander's names--the redhead was Larry he said, and the other's name was Tony, although Stephen was certain he'd heard them refer to each other as Lale and Akoni.

'The fact is they've all got a few names apiece, I reckon,' said Ditler, 'since nobody can ever rightly pronounce their real names they usually get named for their ship, or some kind of humourous nickname that sticks, or they get named for somebody famous. I myself have met an Earl of Sandwich, an Alex the Great, and any number of Ceasars and Kings and Dukes.' He looked down the hill to the beach where they were building a fire and preparing to filet a large thresher shark that two of them had just dragged out of the water and up on to the beach with their bare hands, 'And in a way I'd have to say they *are* kings and dukes, or at least they carry themselves that way, don't they?'

Ditler then explained to Stephen and the others the curious local arrangements for hostelry. Wild horses, it would seem, are in great abundance, and thus a cheap commodity. With even the finest being sold for as little as eighty *reals*, about ten American dollars, the tooled leather saddles are worth more than their mounts.

'So the ostler goes into the hills and catches the horses, usually by clapping on to long ropes tied around their necks for the purpose. Then he rents the saddle and tack for six *reals* a day, the horse being of no great consequence in the bargain.'

Ditler went back down to the Embarcadero and in less than half of an hour the Sandwich Islanders were back with more than enough horses and saddles, still trailing several dogs. The saddles all had unusual stirrups, called *tapaderos*, that enclosed the feet like a large Dutch shoe, and each came with a pair of leather leggings, called *polainas*, which Lale said the Spanish prefer in this country to protect their feet from burrs.

Of the horses one bay mare was so large that a short length of rope had been spliced on the surcingle to reach around her girth. Normally Jack would have chosen her for himself, but he gave over to Fat-Arse Jenks, it being the only mount of the lot that could be expected to bear his mass. Jack was left instead with the second largest, but what turned out after closer examination to be certainly the oldest of the whole lot, which balked and resisted Jack's efforts for the entire time he rode her.

The presidio was about four dusty miles inland; dusty, despite the path being along a riverbank most of the way. The horses fell into an easy rhythm, except for Jack's, and the whole party fell into line, with two additional members, a perpetually smiling black and white border collie, and a little mottled brown and grey shepherd dog, that ran behind Stephen's horse as he engaged Father De La Valle and Jean-Pedro in a turgid Spanish colloquy regarding their modest personal sightings of indigenous fauna. De La Valle's predecessor believed he had seen a grizzly bear one morning near the mission, but when he rang a bell to alert the others it scared the bear away. Both De La Valle and Jean-Pedro had seen puma, of course, as well as many large wolves, several species of snake and lizard, and the curious wild dogs which are common here, called coyotes, that primarily feed on the fecundly ubiquitous rabbits and hares, of which Stephen had already seen thousands just on this ride up from the beach. As for birds, Stephen had already noted three species of duck and two of grouse, terns, finches, thrushes, plovers, swallows and countless black crows. There were flocks of egrets, brown pelican, and innumerable sanderlings, sandpipers, sea gulls and whatnot. And Stephen was told of a flightless bird, not unlike the rail he and Martin had pursued back on Old Sodbury's Island. However, this bird, though said to be capable of short flight, prefers to stay earth-bound and is a very fast runner, called by the Spanish *un carreros-camino*, or the road-runner. Still in all Stephen found it rather barren; where was the 'land of inexpressible fertility' La Perouse had described in his journal?

About three miles inland, dogs still in tow, they passed a sort of small village occupying several low hills all around. Overall there were four rather large houses built in the Spanish-Mediterranean style and painted bright colours. These four were spread out widely and surrounded by handfuls of white or pinkish brown adobe structures all over the hillsides. There were no streets as such, and all the houses were haphazardly facing in any given direction along narrow bridal and foot paths that combed the hills, hardly wide enough for even a small cart.

At length they arrived at the bottom of the large hill on which the Presidio stood along the south bank of the river. They dismounted, Jack most gratefully, and two Indian men made the horses fast to a hitchpost, as the whole entourage, dogs included, ascended afoot to the western side of the fort, toward the main gate, which was located adjacent to a small gun battery.

The Presidio itself was a large square wall made of dried mud and fired brick, and not very sturdy-looking for all that, enclosing about two dozen acres. All around the grounds outside the wall were Indians diligently tilling small plots of various vegetables and herbs, including lima beans, as Jack observed. And it also appeared that on this hard-pan soil with no water source aside from carrying it up the hill they were somehow having much better luck with lima beans than Jack had in his own garden back at Ashgrove Cottage.

Arriving at the gate, Jack was surprised to see it not only was wide open but completely unmanned. Several Indians were sitting against the wall nearby, apparently sleeping with their hats pulled low. A handsome young Indian was leaning rakishly against the gate, looking quite pleased with himself and wearing one over-large leather shoe on his left foot.

All the way around lining the inside of the wall were adjacent buildings: low, stark, whitewashed mud structures with red tile roofs. These were quarters for the Commandant, officers, soldiers, and their families and for the padres, as well as a chapel, grainery, stables, brickmaking facility, smithery, and so forth. In the middle was a sprawling courtyard, the Plaza De Armes, with a pair of flagpoles at its center.

Soldiers in mostly ragged, partial uniforms were lazily milling about in the shade along the periphery of the buildings, mindless of the visitors, as De La Valle led the way across the bright square to the chapel against the south wall. Jean-Pedro followed directly behind De La Valle and then Jack and Stephen and the dogs and the rest behind them. Stephen looked over at Jack's face and could see in its expression his nascent apprehension that De La Valle intended to deal with secular matters second, meaning Jack would first have to endure what would no doubt be a lengthy Catholic religious ceremony, and one in Latin at that, a study which had always caused him to feel inadequate and stupid. As they entered the high-arched doorway to the cool dimly lit chapel vestibule Stephen removed his blue spectacles and looked at Jack, silently mouthing: 'I'm sorry,' with a sympathetic look. Then, just before entering he looked squinting for a moment past Jack to the plaza where something made him smile suddenly, and he gave a cryptic wink before stepping into the shadow.

When Jack first entered the chapel's interior it was redolent of the cypress pine switches which the monks had laid on the floor in a small area used by the Indians, and though this may have proved expedient in shielding the padres' delicate noses from the earthen gaminess of the natives, it would not answer one bit against the likes of a Fat-Arse Jenks just off several months at sea. Jack's eyes were still adjusting to the darkness as the group felt their way along into the pews, and he only realized too late he was sitting directly behind the reeking Jenks. Jack wanted very much to extricate himself from this entire situation, but how? He couldn't think of any acceptable, diplomatic way to avoid attending this Mass in the first place, and even were he not so near the odors source, anywhere in this small, close chapel would prove uncomfortably propinquitous, Jenks' twenty-one stone taking up a sizable portion of the room all of himself. But Jack's seating position also meant he would largely be unable to view the ceremony for what interest it might have to him, or if only to attempt to translate some of the Latin as a distraction from the great odious presence.

Serving for Father De La Valle would be Father Baptisté, now seeming painfully alert, as if brought back from a fainting spell by a bracing dose of camphor salts. Beginning the Mass with a special Spanish welcome, De La Valle blessed the assembled, thoroughly dousing them with his aspugelium, and then proceeded through the codified motions and incantations with a practised efficiency, so that gratefully for everyone, especially Jack, the service was over in less than half of an hour and Jack, Stephen, and De La Valle left to see the Commandant while Jean-Pedro stayed behind and heard penance for the men, starting with Jenks, who spoke Spanish, and who was in and out of the confessional so fast that one of the Catholics, a Pole off *Enderby*, Seaman James Stefanko, heretofore visibly anxious about the possible approbation he might receive for something he would have to share with his confessor, now whispered to Padeen: 'Why, this looks easy as kiss my hand.' And in fact Baptisté could only understand the rudest English, so he conducted the sacrament entirely in Latin and Spanish, just as he did with the Indians, while the rest of the men there all spoke English as softly as their blue water sailor's voices would allow them, so as not to endure looks from their waiting mates upon exiting. The confessor had the least idea of anyone in the room what venial or mortal sins were being confessed to, and of course no one knew what the their penance was, which had the unexpected result of everyone assigning himself a rather harsh one.

Jack, Stephen, and the two dogs followed De La Valle across

the plaza and between two buildings near the southeast corner, finally arriving at the front door of a clean, well-kept two-story cottage-like structure, where De La Valle announced: 'This is the *Commandanté* and Señora Zúñillo's quarters.'

The door opened and there was a young, brown-eyed Indian girl, whose pretty face lit up when she saw the visitors, and she gushed in Spanish: 'Father I am very happy to see you brought visitors! Do they wish to come inside? Who are they, Father? Where do they come from?'

'Where is your clothing, child?' asked De La Valle, ignoring her questions.

She looked down at herself and back up at De La Valle and fecklessly stated that she had merely forgotten to put any on today, and that she would go shift into something now, then she turned and walked away leaving the door to the veranda wide open.

For an awkward moment the three stood at the door, discreetly turning away from the Indian girl, all except Jack, who could not quite restrain himself from stealing a surreptitious glimpse at the graceful movements of her departing limbs.

Presently a tall, handsome-featured Spanish matron came to the door and enthusiastically greeted Father De La Valle:

'*¡Bienvenida! ¡Acger con gusto, Padre De La Valle!*' ('Welcome! A pleasure to receive you, Father De La Valle!')

She stepped back from the door to let them in and De La Valle went into an adjacent room and had a brief conversation in Spanish with the Commandant, then both men joined the lady, the Commandant in a splendid military uniform.

'*Commandanté y Señora Zúñillo*,' said De La Valle with great gravity, 'It is my great honour to present to you Captain Jack Aubrey of the British Royal Navy.'

Jack bowed graciously to the Commandant and showed a respectful leg to the Señora Zúñillo.

'...And his ship's surgeon, Doctor Maturin..' said De La Valle, adding: 'Please excuse me, but I must take my leave and return to the Mission now.'

Stephen, whose demeanor it seemed to Jack had taken on an unusually formal posture for this introduction, showed a graceful leg and said pointedly to Zúñillo:

'*Medico* Esteban Maturin *y* Domanova, *para servir, Mi Commandanté.'*

The Commandant had a flash of recognition flit across his features: 'Why, yes, of course, the Maturin y Domanova of Lérida, yes?'

Jack smiled as it suddenly dawned on him that of the two flagpoles in the Plaza, one was that of Spain, and the other that of Catalonia. The Commandant's colourful uniform was, now that he took note of it, that of the Catalán Volunteers, who, as Jack very well knew and had more or less forgotten, the Spaniards often employ to staff the presidio at many of their far-flung outposts.

'You are from the country of Don Ramón, yes?' asked Zúñillo.

'Indeed,' said Stephen, 'he is my godfather, and my father's particular friend.'

'My cousins live in Lérida, and I spent very much time there as a child,' Zúñillo enthused, 'We are greatly honoured, yes, *very* greatly honoured indeed, to receive the godson of Don Ramón to our humble presidio.' He turned to Jack: 'Captain Aubrey, how many of your officers would you like to invite to a *fiesta* in your honour this evening? There is still plenty of time for the servants, if we get them started now, to prepare a great feast, I assure you. We've been preparing for the festival of *Corpus Christi* next month and have a great deal of foodstuffs on hand. By the way, how large are your two ships, and what fortune brought you here that we can help you with? As you may know, we did have an unfortunate experience with a previous English captain, Captain Brown, but he was a privateer, a blackguard and a thief; not a man of honour, such as you fine gentlemen here.

'How many shall I tell the cooks for dinner? I will send a rider to go fetch your companions and they could easily be here on time for the great meal, yes?'

'How very great and magnanimous in you, *Commandanté*,' said Jack, 'I should like very much to give him a dispatch with the list of names...'

'As many as you like, Captain Aubrey, as many as you like.

It will be a most grand supper, I am sure.'

'Well, perhaps there are about ten men I should wish to so generously reward, with your permission, of course, *Commandanté* Zúñillo.

'As to my ships,' Jack continued, 'We are not merchant men nor anything else of the sort. *Surprise* serves God and King as a man o' war in His Majesty's Navy, and the Enderby is a recaptured prize we're returning with. So we've no inclination toward the hide, nor any other trade for that matter. We are merely hoping to water, take on small stores, allow some rest to the men, and have an uneventful week or two before we catch our tide south to double the Horn. It is to our good fortune that our two great nations are allied together at this time in our mutual struggle against Buonaparte's tyranny.'

'Why that is an excellent toast, Captain,' said Zúñillo, 'Shall I pour us all a glass of wine? No doubt you are both parched from the ride here.'

'That would be splendid,' said Stephen, 'and I wonder if we might tour some of the grounds afterwards. This is the first presidio I have visited.'

'You, Sir, Doctor Maturin,' said Zúñillo, pouring out three glasses with a flourish, 'shall be our honoured guest whenever you visit this presidio during your stay.'

'I greatly look forward to exploring the surrounding area as well, the plants and animals hereabout...' began Stephen, and Jack, grown cheery from the strong local version of Madeirá, interjected:

'Doctor Maturin is a very keen natural philosopher,' Jack was beaming with satisfaction over his friend and their current situation, 'You know, he even discovered a type of tortoise once, and gave it a very pretty Latin name, too, did you not, Stephen?'

Stephen was afraid Jack was perilously close to asking him to tell the one again about the tortoise and the air, so he shifted the subject and asked Zúñillo:

'There is a road we crossed that runs along the coast, do I understand correctly?'

'Yes! That is the King's Road, *El Camino Real*. It connects all the missions in California. And,' he added jovially to Stephen, 'it was of course a Catalán who built it, ha-ha!'

‘Yes,’ said Stephen, ‘That would have been Don Gaspar De Portola, the great explorer of the world, would it not?’

‘Indeed, Esteban, the very same.’ Zúñillo stood up, ‘Come my friends, I will escort you about the Presidio grounds.’

As he led them about, the Commandant rattled away with Stephen in Catalán, while the dogs followed and Jack silently reflected that he had never seen a military post so utterly lacking in discipline as this present one. He learned that one of the fellows sleeping at the gate was in fact the sentry; that the walls were, just as it appeared, utterly crumbling, but it didn’t signify since the Indians were no longer a problem; that some years ago the Indians *had* been a problem, one black night when they burned down the Mission and martyred a monk, and although the flames lit up the night sky, apparently no one on ‘duty’ that night at the nearby Presidio even noticed; and he learned that the small battery they saw by the gate as they came in had three guns: a ridiculous carronade with it’s carriage broken, and two long guns, one of which had been spiked Jack noted, and besides, it was plain that none of the roundshot present would fit any of the three guns, even if they could be made to fire.

Zúñillo’s position here, Jack gathered, was something of a clack-handed sinecure, since it seemed to Jack that more than anything else the Commandant was terribly lonely at his frontier post, and though he favored a proper and formal demeanor for himself, he was clearly unable to evoke it in his own men who usually even failed to evince proper respect toward rank as they passed. The real work at the Presidio was handled mostly by the Indians, and Zúñillo himself volunteered at one point that the real military work was usually handled by a battery of eight excellent brass nine-pounders on carriages, with plentiful ball as well as chain shot. The Spaniards had built it, stocked it, and manned it themselves on Guijarros Point, on the tall cliff *Surprise* had sailed under, just south of the bay upon arrival.

The Catholics were all sent back with the courier, all except Jenks, who spoke some Spanish, and whom the monks were given to have stay at the mission across the river and begin work tomorrow on the aqueduct. When the invited *Surprises* from the ship arrived with the returning courier, everyone was extremely sharp-set.

Given in Zúñillo's home, the meal proved as palatable as promised. Besides a unique local version of succotash made combining the lima beans Jack had noted with crushed maize, there was a kind of crowdy the Indians made by crushing up pine nuts and native esculent plants with a bit of tallow added, into a gruel sauce. There were plentiful grapes, olives, lemons and oranges, as well as pumpkins, yams, eggplant, varieties of melons and squash, and the local beans, called *frijoles fritos*, which everyone agreed were by far the best they had ever eaten. As for meats, they had some very good salted beef and pork, as well as fresh venison and, of course, abundant roast hare.

'What is this delightful meat dish here?' asked Jack, savoring a piece, 'Capital flavour!' He tried a bit more, 'as good as turtle meat! Delicious! Pray, what animal is it?'

'Rattlesnake,' replied Zúñillo.

As the cloth was at last withdrawn, Zúñillo stood up, a bit waveringly, held his glass high and looked at Stephen to his right and smiled very warmly, then he turned to the rest of the table, aglow in cordiality, and said:

'*Que no haya novedad.*' ('May no new thing arise.')

'To all our good fortunes, and to the devil for Buonaparté!'

He turned back to Stephen and said:

'Esteban, toast with me; to the devil with Phillip *de Cinco*, and God bless Count Borrell!'

Stephen raised his glass along with the rest of the table, and everyone, Catalán or no, gave a great cheer and slaked a hearty drink to Count Borrell.

Afterwards, everyone retired to the large stone *patio* courtyard and parterre adjacent to Zúñillo's house where there were musicians and dancers, and a score or so of prominent citizenry who had come to this impromptu social event to welcome the visitors. The dancers wore very tight fitting colourful costumes, and their motions and their expressions as they danced, especially the men's, were extremely severe and dramatic, with a great deal of rapid staccato rapping of the heels to the floor to punctuate things. The local women in general appeared unusually endowed with good looks, but the women dancers were exceptional beauties, very fetching in the corsetted dresses that spun with them as they danced the *sardana* around the singer, a fiery-eyed raven-haired vixen who clicked a pair of *castañeta* as she danced and struck beautiful poses, while behind the dancers the clouds lifted and revealed the moon, reflected in the ocean water miles away down the hill.

'Esteban Maturin, godson of Don Ramón,' said Zúñillo, approaching Stephen with an extremely handsome and richly dressed couple, 'It is my supreme privilege to present to you a friend of the King, and a distinguished *gente de razon*, Don Onofre De Las Pulgas, and his lovely wife, Doña-Fior.'

By this time Stephen was becoming inured to the grandiloquent formal introductions favoured here, but looking up at Doña-Fior while kissing her hand he was momentarily startled by her implausibly arresting beauty, and a sudden unexpected wave of melancholy swept over his mind as thoughts of Diana secretly pierced him. Thoughts that filled him with a sense of helpless anxiety. A world away, as part of his intelligence work he had unfortunately contrived to give an erroneous impression he was being brazenly indiscreet. He had written her a letter of some explanation and given it to an associate, Andrew Wray, to deliver, hoping it would reach her before the rumours, but it didn't answer. Part of the reason he welcomed this voyage had been to push her from his mind, and until now he had largely succeeded.

But now, with Doña-Fior's fine features and dark gaunt beauty, so like Diana's, standing here before him, her brave eyes, not blue but sea-green, deep-set and proud, like Diana's, and set dead on Stephen's; her very breath was sweet, and with each inspiration her gravid breasts threatened to burst from her décolleté gown, just inches from Stephen's nose, with the whole effect of it to suddenly make Diana, though across the other side of the world, seem palpably, painfully present.

'Doctor Maturin,' Don Onofre embraced Stephen like a long lost brother, 'you must do me the honour of coming to my rancho for dinner one evening while you are here. You would be our first Catalán guest, save for the *Commandanté* and members of the Volunteers, of course. I would like very much to have an informed discussion of foreign affairs with such worldly men as yourself and the Captain.'

'Don Onofre has the very finest estate, Esteban,' said Zúñillo, 'Rancho Soledad is the finest land in *Nueva California*, as anyone will attest.'

'A wonderful gift from His Majesty which I humbly accepted stewardship of,' said Don Onofre, 'and it would please me greatly if you could extend the invitation to your Captain, Jack Aubrey, for me?'

'Why yes,' said Stephen absently, 'he's my particular friend. I'm sure we would both be delighted to attend, if duty allows, of course.'

'Do you think perhaps Sunday yourself and the Captain could attend?'

'I shall have to ask Jack, but for myself it would be fine, yes.'

'Good. Sunday it is, until you tell me otherwise. Any Indian will run a message to me because they know I pay a *real* for messages sent to me, and two *reals* for messages sent back.'

'Don Onofre,' said Stephen, hoping to clear his head by distancing himself from Doña-Fior's perfume, 'Let me fetch Jack from across the way and I shall introduce you and we can confirm the arrangement right now.'

When he reached Jack it was the first private moment between them since they'd arrived, and Jack took the opportunity to practise upon Stephen.

'By God, Stephen,' he said flatly, 'I must say I expected a bit more of you as a diplomat; you've made an awful cock of things here for us.'

'And don't be over-estimating it now, either, Jack. I don't actually speak Catalán quite as well as once I did, though in the next day or so I expect I shall.

'But listen, Jack, I'm going to introduce you to this local sort of baron, he and his wife appear crashing bores, but it looks like on Sunday he'll be entertaining us at his rancho, and there's no escaping it for us.' With that Stephen began to lead him across the *patio* toward Don Onofre and Doña-Fior.

Jack whispered: 'That very, very handsome couple that you were just speaking, Stephen, they are the bores, are they?'

Don Onofre was wearing a close-stitched suit that was a tailor's masterpiece, and completed the sartorial assemblage with a long pizzle for a walking stick, while Doña-Fior's entire *ensemblé*, shoes, gown, and broach, were all *dernier cri*.

'Excuse me, you are right, Jack: they are a fresh sight for sour eyes, are they not? Perhaps I've presumed to judge.'

'Well,' said Jack, 'boring or not, by Sunday I should certainly be ready for another magnific meal like this evening's was.'

Chapter Six

The following morning a splendid breakfast was provided by the padres of eggs, rice, *frejoles fritos*, and a delicious type of corn crumpet called *tortillas*. Afterward, with the two dogs still shadowing Stephen, all the *Surprises* set out on horseback for the ship except Fat-Arse Jenks, who was staying at the mission, and whose horse Jack now gratefully used instead for the downhill ride to the ship. Stephen arrived at the beach first and was met by the two Sandwich Islanders, Lale and Akoni. The two bitches careered wildly down the bluffs to Lale, the border collie barking and the smaller cattle shepherd yelping in utter joy, both wagging frantically.

'No biting, Keiki Hae,' said Lale, dismounting as the shepherd leapt and nipped at him. 'Where have my little *amigas* been hiding?' He stroked the border collie's coat, 'Someplace where you were fed, your belly looks full Náenáe, ha-ha!'

'*Hehena káia* Keiki Hae!' said Akoni, laughing very hard and pointing as the shepherd continued her joyous leaping.

Lale was laughing as well, and the harder he laughed the more excited Keiki Hae became. He explained to the arriving Stephen, nodding toward Akoni: 'He called Keiki Hae here crazy, like they call the Indian, Luis Loco; everyone has been wondering where he and Keiki Hae and Náenáe have been since yesterday.

'But I see my little friends have attached themselves to you.'

'I was indeed thus honoured by the dear creatures,' said Stephen.

'They are my little canine *aikáne*, they befriended me one day just the same as they did you, so we are all *aikáne* now!' he said laughing, and added, 'I'm Lale, and this is Akoni, but the *ha'oles* sometimes call us Larry and Tony, if you prefer that.'

'Oh I much prefer Lale and Akoni, if that's all right.'

'Of course you do! You are *aikáne*!' Lale put his fingers to his cheek and rubbed his skin, 'And you are no *ha'ole*, are you? Are you *kanaka*?'

'No, I've just tanned in the sun like one of your hides, I'm afraid. And do all the *kanakas* speak such good English?'

Lale and Akoni burst out laughing at this and Lale, affecting an impeccable Etonic dialect, said:

'Oh, you *flahter* me, my good man, but it so happens I was *tawght* English at a very young age.'

Akoni was now nearly hysterical at Lale's impersonation of an Englishman, but he gasped: 'All *kanakas* know English! '

'Well, this is true,' said Lale, in mock sheepishness, 'And I practise my English reading and writing quite a bit with books that I obtain, but most of the *kanakas* prefer to speak our own tongue; it's a very poetic sort of language, you know. But I'm afraid it's true all the *kanakas* know at least a bit of English; after all, it's not for nothing they call the Sandwich Islands the "Venice of the Pacific."'

'Do they call them that, then?' said Stephen, 'I hadn't heard that before this.'

'Oh yes,' said Lale spreading his arms out wide, 'we *kanakas* know about every little thing occurring in the great world, don't we Akoni?' and they both began laughing again.

'Well, I don't believe I introduced myself, my name is Stephen Maturin--'

Lale's eyes widened, 'Doctor Stephen Maturin? The esteemed medical writer?' He turned to Akoni and pointed at Stephen, saying:

'*Kákau puke oia*!'

It was almost as if Stephen were being practised upon, but Lale's pure earnest nature was incapable of it.

'You're familiar with my work, then?'

'Only one of your books, though I know you have written others as well. The surgeon of the old *Lelia Bird* traded me a copy of *Tar-Water Revisited* for a fine pearl some years ago, and I read the whole book, too, but, alas, I think I only understood but a little bit of it.'

'And now you *flahter* me, do you not?' asked Stephen, turning around to the others who were arriving behind him, 'This is Captain Jack Aubrey, and, Jack, this is Lale and Akoni, two of the many English speaking Sandwich Islanders,' Stephan smiled, 'Lale here has read one of my books, Jack.'

'I still have my copy of it, Doctor,' Lale revealed his large white teeth.

'Please to call me Stephen, if you would, Lale.'

Akoni said: 'I wish to call you Doctor, if I may impose. One *kanaka*, Lopaka, needs a doctor to view him. Maybe you come, yes?'

'Yes,' added Lale, 'It would be most excellent in you if you could come down to the hide house some day while you are here and look at Lopaka, he's been very sick for most of the day.'

'I shall do just that tomorrow,' said Stephen, 'and then I hope to explore some of the points of interest to a natural philosopher in this area. Would you be familiar with such places, Lale?'

'I shall take you to where the humourous trees grow on the beach and the cliffs if you like.'

'Humourous trees, you say?'

'Down-side up trees!' exclaimed Akoni, smiling.

'Yes,' said Lale, 'many of them do grow upside-down. I could easily take you there, after you so kindly tend to Lopaka.'

'I'm not at all sure I'll be able to help, but I certainly will try'

But before Stephen could debark *Surprise* in the morning he was required to spend some unpleasant time checking the intromittent organs of all the day's shorebound men, in this case all the first watch larbowlins, for any possible signs of gleet. This, despite the facts that in the town there was nary a knocker's shop nor a shebeen to be found, and that the local husbands and brothers were known to be murderously jealous, making prospects for amorous unions seemingly remote. At this port there had been no bum-boats loaded with whores for Captain Aubrey to dismiss on their arrival, as was the case in so many other ports, for here anyone intending to remain permanently as a resident was required to convert to Roman Catholicism. And although the women isolated in this frontier settlement seemed improbably attractive, they were also for the most part spoken for, and, of course, Captain Aubrey had been plain that the Indian women were strictly off limits. Nonetheless, shore leave here offered good riding, hunting, and eating, and some socializing in the town where there was a small, one-room, mud grog-shop, which, besides liqueurs, sold dry and west India goods, shoes, bread, fruits, and everything else vendible in California.

Martin was engaged with the still weak Captain Palmer and thus unable to accompany Stephen to see the trees, but in fact Martin had little interest in them, when all around him was a gushing abundance of all the grallatorres birds--cormorants, curlews, brown pelicans, ring plovers, and the ethereal snowy egret, *egretta thula*--and when glancing ashore he could see almost no trees at all, humourous or elsewise, looking clear to the hilltops.

Stephen, on the other hand, found himself both fascinated with the prospect of the California wilderness, and intrigued by his unusually winsome guide. Setting off on foot for the hide houses, he was met halfway by Lale, Akoni, and the two excited dogs who greeted Stephen as if he had risen from the dead. Náenáe, the border collie, her face in an unmistakable smile, squirmed all around Stephen's ankles, looking up at him with her head held low in supplication, while she wagged so vigorously her whole body bent back and forth with each stroke of her tail. Keiki Hae, the little cattle shepherd, jumped up and down, up and down, all the while nipping at the shoulders of Stephen's paletot, eventually succeeding in knocking the laughing Stephen to the ground, where both dogs tried to lick his face until Stephen's wig fell off and Keiki Hae ran off with it in her mouth.

Lale called to her in a strong voice and she dropped the wig and stood panting and smiling, dutifully awaiting further orders. Náenáe trotted over, gingerly picked up the wig in her teeth, and brought it over to lay it gently down at Stephen's feet.

'Náenáe giveth what Keiki Hae taketh away!' said Lale, as Stephen put it back on, 'And the truth is, Náenáe often retrieves items like this for me that I didn't even know Keiki Hae had stolt!'

Arriving at the hide houses, Akoni led Stephen to a pair of very large ovens, neither of which was in use, except as a living quarters for some of the Sandwich Islanders. Akoni asked a young boy of about fifteen:

'Kiristopa, *Aia i hea ó* Lopaka?'

'He asked, "Where is Lopaka,"' explained Lale, and Christopher here says Lopaka is feeling better and went out.

'I'm sorry, Doctor, for wasting your time, he really was very ill yesterday but it turns out he only ate some bad shellfish. Lakoni knows better than to eat the dark clams in these waters this time of the year—we dove for pearls together in Baja California in the year two, and he knew better then. But fishing wasn't going well yesterday and he got hungry, he said.'

'Are there many decopods—that is to say shellfish, hereabouts then?'

'Plenty enough not to eat the wrong ones, but to be sure only a handful of different kinds, and most are very small, at least compared to home. There is one larger clam, the Indians call it "Heliotes," they taste very good cooked and the shells clean up to a pretty shiny greenish mother 'o pearl; here, one of these…' Lale bent over and picked up an oval–shaped shell about twelve inches across, from the floor by the oven hearth.

'It's exquisite,' said Stephen, examining the wavy striations of iridescent yellows, blues and greens.

'I can show you many more things of interest along the way to *punta de los arboles*, which is what the Spaniards call the humourous trees. It's about a five leagues ride and then some hiking, so if we get about it now we shall have plenty of time, Stephen. But may I call you by your island name, "Tepano," *aikáne*? It means "Stephen."'

'You are very good. And I hope to hear more of your language as well while we are here.'

'Oh, if that's the case I shall see if Akoni and Kiristopa wish to come along with us; those two prattle all day long.'

Keiki Hae was happily running in and out of the hide house in gleeful anticipation of the ride, while Náenáe sat bolt upright by the doorway like a sentry. They both followed Lale out to the back where he had two horses tied.

'Akoni and Kiristopa have gone ahead to find horses, and may only be able to join us for the ride home, I'm afraid,' said Lale. 'Luis Loco, the hostler, still hasn't been seen, and with Luis there is no accounting…it's not for nothing they call him "Loco."'

For the first few miles of the ride they adhered strictly to El Camino Real because, as Lale explained, the mission valley Indians thought it was bad luck to kill rattlesnakes, with the unintended result that it was in fact now bad luck for you or your horse, or your dogs, to stray into this brush, and very bad luck indeed to be thrown from one of these essentially wild horses which will then bolt and leave you, perhaps with a broken leg or snake-bitten, in a scorching sun.

'And speaking of getting bitten, take care with some of the cacti in this country,' said Lale, 'Don't let your horse bump you into one of the greater ones, and don't you or your horse step on certain of the smaller ones. Do you see that?'

Lale pointed to a squat round plant with green and yellow striped leaves about six inches long pointing out from the center in a starburst pattern.

'Don't ever dismount and step on one of those blasted little things. The leaves are quite sharp and rigid—they call them "Spanish Bayonettes."'

'Oh, yes, of course,' said Stephen, '*Yucca lanciolate*, if I am not mistaken.'

'If you are stung by anything, however,' Lale pointed to a somewhat similar looking green plant growing along the edge of the other side of El Camino Real, 'break these leaves open and there's medicine inside.'

'It happens I'm familiar with the aloe plant as well,' said Stephen, adding: 'not to be confused, of course, with the pungent medicinal we call aloe and sulphure, which doctors sometimes use to help balance the humours.'

The two continued on in silence, the dogs following, along another mile or two of the scrub chapparel landscape, past small stands of pepper and scrub-oak trees, and vast fields of fennel, nettle, sage, and goldenrod, sprinkled with countless species of wild flowers, some amazing in their beauty, only visited by the occasional transient trespass of a peripatetic Russian thistle. At length they left the road in a northwesterly direction and, following what Stephen thought to be either deer trails or Indian trails, gradually entered a shallow valley between a large hill to the east and a tall, sheer, one hundred foot bluff overlooking the Pacific to the west. There was a hint of foggy haze over the water, and in general it was not nearly so parched looking as the rest of the ride had seemed. Indeed, before them now, half a mile away in a mist, was a green pasture with several bullocks visible grazing and a gulp of magpies circling overhead.

'That is the Rancho Soledad,' said Lale, and as he pointed at it both dogs began running as fast as ever they could toward the pasture.

'Oh,' said Stephen, 'It happens I'll be back here again on Sunday.'

Looking at Stephen's expression Lale said: 'You don't wish to go there, Tepano?'

'I will just say that I would much prefer to occupy my mind with natural philosophy than certain inane social obligations and all their weary accompanying compunctions.' Despite their short acquaintance and his normally reticent, very private nature, Stephen felt comfortable returning Lale's genuine, open candidness.

'Oh, I understand you, Tepano,' Lale smiled, 'And I think I can help you, if you will follow me now.'

Lale rode down toward the pasture, and when he saw a white lily along the path, with nonchalant aplomb he hung down from his horse using only his legs to clap on, plucked the lily from the ground, held it to his nose briefly, placed it behind his car, and then just as casually and deftly pulled himself back astride again before Keiki Hae could get back to nip at him, since she thought he was playing a game with her. When they arrived at the pasture he rode to a spot by a large pepper tree and got off his horse, Stephen and the dogs joining him.

'Do you see it?' he asked smiling slyly, as if Stephen were in on his joke.

He bent down, and on the ground in front of him was a chip of cow dung with some small, cap-headed mushrooms growing on it. Lale held one of the lily's petals under one of the fungi and tapped on its' head. From its' reddish underside it released a splotch of purplish-brown spores. Lale examined the flower petal and nodded.

'These are very good mushrooms to eat,' Lale was grinning with his large teeth.

'That is *psilicibus cubensus* if I am not mistaken,' said Stephen.

'That is a very pretty *hao'le* name, Tepano, but did you ever eat them?'

'I have never, no. But I've read some of the journals of the aesthete gymnosophists who have used such mushrooms, as well as the more dangerous *amanita muscarita* and the Mazatecas' *pipiltzinzintli*; and sure, riding here today I spotted a variety of plants that will yield *datura*, as well as a great many *lophophora williamsii*, which they also used copiously, but strictly for religious purposes, of course.'

'Of course. Tepano, you are a wise *aikáne*, but on this Lale is wise: the jimsom weed and the cactus of the Indians is *maika'i 'ole*; no good. It even makes the Indians sick. These do not.'

'Well, the esteemed James Lind, the great authority of the world on ergot intoxication happens to agree with you, Lale, for he also wrote extensively and favorably regarding the *psilicybi* fungus, which he considered akin to a magical philter.' Stephen removed a small gallipot from his bag, 'Here, give them to me then, and I shall crush them apart for us.'

While they were washing down the mushrooms with water, Lale took out a tinder box and a small, powerful scrutineers glass, along with a chillum pipe packed with cured pistillate cannabis flowers. Using the glass and tinder he lit the chillum and inhaled very deeply, holding the smoke in for as long as possible. When at last he exhaled he handed the pipe to Stephen.

'Take a big "Oahu" puff, Tepano, so the mushrooms answer properly.'

Stephen took a large puff in his mouth, but was surprised by the smokes harshness upon inhaling it, and he blew it out in a coughing, sputtering exhalation.

'If nothing else that is a fine expectorant I find,' said Stephen, when he had at last regained himself.

Lale suppressed a laugh and said: 'Little bit slower, Tepano,' and then, looking past Stephen with alarm he shouted: '*Cave canem*! Don't let Keiki Hae …'

Stephen turned and saw the dog's tongue licking up the leftovers in the gallipot, then she ran off to pester the bullocks with Náenáe giving chase.

'No, Keiki Hae, no!' called Lale, but she paid him no heed whatsoever.

Stephen looked quizzically at the islander, 'Lale, you said: "Beware of Dog," did you not? You have the Latin then?'

Lale smiled, and with his eyes twinkling, looked at Stephen and recited:

'*Sucipiat Dominus sacraficium de minibus tuis, ad laudem et gloriam nominis sui, ad utilitatem quoque nostrum, totiusque ecclesiae suæ sanctæ.*'

Stephen smiled at Lale's perfect rendering of the ancient acolyte's tongue twister and exclaimed: 'You astonish me, Lale!'

Lale had got the tinder going and lit the chillum again, placing it in Stephen's hand and saying: 'Not too much at once, Tepano.

'I know that Latin prayer because my father taught it to me; my adopted father that is. He is the one who taught me English very young, and he is partly why I have so many names.'

'So many names?' asked Stephen as he expelled the smoke, having this time tolerated it quite well.

'Yes. "Lale" is just a sort of *kanaka* sobriquet, because sometimes I like to do things fast—I talk fast, ride fast, swim fast—so they call me "Lale-Uile" which means something like greased lightening in English. But part of the reason for "Lale" is it's short for my formal *kanaka* name, which is Lauleneke Kahuliohana, although that isn't my original *kanaka* name.'

'It isn't…?' mumbled Stephen.

'No. You see, my mother died abirthing and my father,

unfortunately, was one of a dozen *kanakas* from Kau'ai who were killed in retaliation for Captain Cook. I was a very small child in seventy-nine and I was adopted by a priest who lived on Kau'ai and named me after himself, "Lawrence Cahalan." He is the reason I know the *Sucipiat*,' smiled Lale, 'He taught it to me. But I won't practise upon you, *aikáne*, I don't really have Latin, just the Mass and a few phrases, but of course he taught me English and Spanish at a very early age.'

'He sounds like a very learned fellow to be in such remote parts.'

'He was a Jesuit, you see; a Pelagian Jesuit. He had lived at the mission at Loreto, just a way south of here—not far from where Lopaka and I would dive for pearls many years later. When the Society of Jesus was expelled by the Spaniards and Franciscans he escaped aboard a Russian whaler to the Islands,' Lale gave Stephen a conspiratorial wink, 'I don't tell this story to Father De La Valle, God love him, ha-ha!'

Stephen sat, fascinated by Lale's tale, hardly noticing the gradually warming feeling the mushrooms and cannabis were bringing to his mind, and Lale continued.

'He worked every day and every hour that God sent, and he taught me everything he could manage to cram into my little island brain. He called it my opportunity to learn English and the *hoa'le* ways in "all their nuance and subtlety," to use a favourite phrase of his.'

'Well thank the dear he didn't turn you to an atheist.'

'Oh, not at all, Tepano, never in life! But unfortunately he cut himself on some coral and died when I was about ten, and that's when I was taken to the Big Island and adopted by some family relations called Kahuliohana, which, believe me or don't, sounds just like Cahalan to a *kanaka* anyway!' Lale laughed very hard at his own joke, and went on:

'But I am *ehu*, you see?' Lale pointed to his red hair.

'What does this mean?' asked Stephen.

'Redheads like me are called *ehu*, from the old legends of Keei, on the south Kona coast of the biggest Sandwich Island, which is called Hawai'i. It is told that a ship wrecked there long ago and a red-headed *hoa'le* couple survived; all the *ehu* are said to have descended from these two.'

'Red-headed mariners,' said Stephen, slowly bringing his hand to his chin, 'Why, they were probably the ancient Celts; we may be distant cousins, Lale!' and they both laughed very hard as a contented euphory swept over Stephen, and for a moment all the great world and all the great sweep of time seemed coherent, comprehensible, concatenate; concordant.

They rode the horses a short distance to the northwest and Lale pointed to a gnarled, scrubby-looking pine tree.

'There is one of the humourous trees, but this one isn't growing in the sort of improbable location that most of them pick to take root. It's not very humourous really.' But Lale laughed anyway.

They tied the horses to it and proceeded on foot.

'We must go north of this spot and I can find the path. This mound is a place for the Indian dead.'

At last they came to a large arroyo running down, down and down to a ridge where they padded across a fallen tree trunk, and then skittered along a very steep, sandy bluff about twenty feet above a small stream whose gurgling sounds came up through the small crack at the top and echoed across the rock face. Coming to a large sandstone boulder they wended their way down through an eighteen inch wide crack in it and came out on the bottom on the other side where the stream to the right turned to a waterfall, spashing down fifteen yards into a rock grotto and continuing toward the sea.

'I need to cut some of this Spanish reed while we are here today,' said Lale, stopping at a long cane break of *arundo donax*. After very carefully selecting several culms he finally cut a three foot length from one of them and placed it in his bag. He then cut several tall stout stalks and laid them by the path to pick up on the way back.

'I promised the Indian children I would bring them some canes,' explained Lale, 'They make spears and hoops from them and play a deer hunting game called "takersia."'

'And the smaller piece?' asked Stephen.

'Oh, that one is for me, for my clarionet. I must age the piece I cut today; it will be clarionet reeds for next year,' said Lale, smiling.

'You play music as well, Lale? You amaze me, brother.'

'Oh yes, Tepano, Father Lawrence taught me to read music,

and years ago I aquired an excellent French clarionet from Captain Crampon of the *Fountáinpierre.*'

'Well, myself and Captain Aubrey often play music together in the evenings, he on his violin and I on my violincello. Perhaps you would join us some evening while we are here. I'm sure Jack would be delighted.'

Stephen was smiling with such joy of the day that his cheeks were actually beginning to pleasantly ache. He was standing at the edge of the bluff looking out to sea at the passing clouds, when a pair of ravens appeared right at his feet, hovering on the wind current along the cliff face. The one nearest Stephen explored the buoyant breeze by spreading out his wing tips and slowly opening and closing them, like some coy, corvine gambler with a hand of piquet. Stephen studied the corbins' motions for several minutes, and as they played upon the wind they remained remarkably close to Stephen, as if keeping him company. He looked out across the ocean and it's shroud of mammatis clouds again, and the entire cast of the welkin had shifted to a study in blue hues from periwinkle through cyan, to a deep violet at the horizon's edge. Looking at a small bush growing out of the bluffside, it looked like even the stems beneath the foliage were a sort of slate blue-grey. He noticed how viscous the surface of the water appeared, glittering like a rough cut diamond, while the colour of simply everything around seemed wonderfully vivid.

Certainly, thought Stephen, colours must always be so, but life's hum-drum concerns cause one to become dull, insensible of it. Though Stephen often had only the meanest apprehension of colours, in his current state of mind even looking at the most mundane things rewarded with a rich, vibrant palette. Indeed, the staggering beauty of the clouds before him now was truly humbling.

And how improbable were clouds to begin with, wondered Stephen? From a natural philosopher's perspective, how queer and implausible a thing are these ephemeral, nebulous puffs of air? Whether part of some teleological plan, or random result of nature's laws, infinite in supply and variety, they float in the heavens of their own accord, and can only be observed, like a forest or a great battle, when one is at a goodly distance, as the closer one gets, the more ill-defined become the boundaries of the thing; yet for all their amorphous and quaint singularity, how fortunate for man that he can take their sheer beauty for granted? Why, after all, should clouds not be ugly? Certainly many of nature's handiworks are, and for all of creation that isn't Stephen had never before felt so grateful. He had rarely paid a great deal of attention to clouds before, but today was certainly different. Today Stephen wondered if this wasn't the way Gainsborough or Briggs saw the world around them every day; so phantasmagoric, refulgent and sparkling, and of a moment so mortal and so priceless. He resolved to try and recreate the effect when not under the encorcelling influence of the *psilsibi*.

The ravens flew off to the north and Lale pointed in their direction and said: 'The black birds will accompany us to the humourous trees; there they are.'

Stephen looked along the bluff and down to the beach, and assessed the area where the strangely shaped pine trees were rooted in very sandy soil and sculpted by the prevailing winds. Thus, when they reached a given height the loose-packed earth would lose its' tenuous grip, the tree would lose its' precarious balance, and down it would go. But despite toppling, they usually continued to grow, with those near the bluff edge in many cases growing completely inverted, as fore-claimed.

Upon closer examination of the trees they appeared to Stephen to be a rare sort of white or yellow pentamorous needled pine, with the unusual capacity to extract moisture they need from the briny coastal fog. Though hardly neoteric, still they were rare, and probably not yet named, but Stephen's knowledge of botanical taxonomy was not sufficient to determine for sure. If they produced any interesting strobili it was too late in the season for any to be seen, but there were in evidence hecatombs of very large pine cones, the nuts of which were also large; as large as the biggest pinion pine's, although these humourous trees themselves were quite diminutive by comparison.

'The Indians have a place they go sometimes at low tide,' said Lale, 'where they grind up the nuts on the reef to make food.'

'I believe I sampled some at last evening's supper,' said Stephen, 'they're not unlike in appearance to the well-known *simmondia californica*, or goat nut, that Archibald Menzies praised for it's medicinal value.'

'That is a splendid drawing you are doing, Tepano,' said Lale, looking at Stephen's notes, 'It looks like the very thing itself.'

'Well, it's rather rude, really, but thank you for saying so,' said Stephen with genuine modesty, 'I've been trying to improve my renderings of late and today my eyes are amazingly good.'

Lale flashed his enormous teeth and said: 'I will leave you here to study awhile, and when you are ready to start back, come and fetch me.'

'Where will you be?'

'I will be about a half of a mile south along the beach, you will see me swimming just off the shore. You can hail me, or if you like join me in the water,'

'No, thank you, Lale, I'm not a particularly good swimmer, I find, but I will meet back up with you shortly.'

Chapter Seven

Finishing his drawing, Stephen carefully wended his way down the rest of the bluff to the beach, collecting some very interesting beetles and insects along the way, including an enormous, shiny, black and yellow striped wingless cricket the size of a field mouse. There were also at least two species of lizard, either nervously scurrying under foot or blissfully oblivious, basking in the warm sand. The baby lizards could be readily scooped up in a handful of sand and let to run a few circles before leaping away. Pestering the adults, however, could cause them to rear up on hind quarters, hissing and snapping like angry snakes.

Down and down, following in Lale's tracks until at last he was standing in the deep baking sand. A cooling mist from the breakers about seventy-five yards out hung in the balmy air above the broad beach, where large boils of fragile looking seabirds ran tirelessly up and down the shoreline following the lapping of the ocean, and hunting for tiny crabs. On top of the bluff, and also climbing down it, it had been rather breezy. But now, here at sea level, the air had a stillness and comfort unlike any Stephen had ever known, and he stood for a moment to enjoy it. To the north he saw a murmuration of at least two score of brown pelicans, or *alcatraz*, as the Spaniards here call them, with their huge wings, gliding silently across the sky as one. As he watched they flew eastward, putting the tawny bluff behind them, and in doing so, completely disappeared. Looking south, in the direction of Lale's footprints, a sandy beach nearly one quarter mile in breadth stretched along and perhaps all the way around a rocky point about four miles distant. Foreshortening his focus a bit, Stephen saw a long piece of Spanish reed planted like a flag in the sand a few hundred yards away, with Lale's hat and shirt perched atop it. Walking towards it, Stephen looked into the surf and saw Akoni and Kiristopa bathing in the surging waters along with Lale. When they noted Stephen was watching they began showing away with great amusement, all three laughing at each other's capers like a pack of carefree popinjays, often as massive combers broke mere inches away from them with a fearsome basso thump.

Stephen sat in the shade of Lale's shirt and squinted out at the white foamy soup, carefully observing their motions as the powerful swimmers made their way about in the roiling waters. They waited, facing out to sea, until a wave or group of waves, one close upon the next, began to form. Jockeying for position by any means possible, each one sought to place himself exactly where the next insipient wave was about to break. As it did, they would turn and begin swimming with the wave in an amazing hand over hand fashion going toward, but also somewhat parallel to, the shore. As the lip of the comber formed it found them poised at the shoulder's apex where they would stop stroking, and, almost standing still for a suspended moment, they would extend their forward arm like a steering oar and place their hand upon the stretched face of the water. As they did this the jacking wave brought their feet up above their heads and with a powerful kick they would swoop down the face of the curling breaker with great celerity. Once in the trough they would ride along just ahead of the peeling wave, laughing and hallooing back and forth wildly. They did this over and over, sometimes in the larger seas getting pitched a goodly distance through the air, often landing ignominiously face first. Whenever this happened they would invariably emerge from the foamy chaos laughing or making faces at their companions before pursuing the next smoking wave. Smoking, because the comber's leading edge released a wonderfully fine misty spray into the breeze, which had now turned offshore, making all the waves look as if they were afire.

Stephen sat in a complacent, happy stupor, a thoughtless state of mind, and he found it a rare good spirit that stayed with him through the afternoon. He had at some point fallen asleep, however, since the laughter of Akoni and Kiristopa had just awakened him, and he sat up blinking in the bright sun as they approached soaking wet across the hot sand. Lale's voice came from behind him:

'We will have to go back north to fetch our horses, Tepano, but we will meet Akoni and Kiristopa on the clifftop.'

Neither spoke as they walked atop the hard-packed sand at the water's edge; Lale's mind was in repose after his long swim, and Stephen's was still groggily sorting through the real from the dreamed experiences of the day. His dreams had not looked or seemed in any particular way real, but some of today's real sights and experiences now seemed in retrospect rather dreamlike: the improbable coastal pine trees, weather growing more perfect with each passing hour, the well-behaved 'wild' horses, and the ride through a desert terrain so bristling with a plenitude of cacti that the landscape appears out of focus for it. And then there were the Sandwich Islanders with all their capering in the surf, wondrously moving through the water like nypholepts, fearless and filled with joy… all the way back to the horses Stephen recalled how they had soared about, sometimes almost seeming as birds in flight. But no, he had not dreamed most of it, most of it had been quite real.

Up, up and up they climbed, Stephen's calves were burning now, his knees were beginning to ache, and his breathing was very heavy, though Lale up ahead was going much faster with no apparent effort. Indeed, with a discernable spring in his step all the way to the top. There, he looked back at the sea, took a very deep breath of air, exhaled and said:

'*Viento desierte*, *aikáne, Viento desierte*! We must come back here tomorrow!'

When Stephen finally arrived on top he stood bent over with his hands on his knees, gasping for breath and said:

'I find the air has changed, has it not?' He stood up straight, putting his arms akimbo and, sticking out his chest to catch his last bit of breath, he absently gazed off the cliff down to the sea.

'Yes, Tepano, *Viento desierte*, the desert winds, and right now the surfing is sweet, what we call *maika'i ná nalu*, and the wind helps to shape these waves just so, the better for the *kanakas* to ride upon them, ha-ha! Akoni and I often come here, because it is known by all *kanakas* to be the very best beach of San Diego for riding of the waves. You see, the reef, if there is one, is buried deep in the sand, so it doesn't cut you. There are no large submerged rocks either, and the water is nice and deep, what sailors sometimes call steep-to. The waves today were breaking in about three fathoms, but a short swim past that point and you're out of soundings, very deep. We're used to waves like that. Very nice waves today, maybe nicer still tomorrow,' he said, smiling with his big teeth.

'I give you joy of it,' said Stephen, laughing, I was truly amused, if not to say amazed, by all your capering. But do you not worry about sharks?'

Lale burst out laughing and said:

'You've gotten in backward, *aikáne*, the sharks must worry about us, but unfortunately we don't see that many to catch.'

This last remark jostled Stephen's memory back to the only other time he had observed anyone swimming in the swift fashion that Lale and his friends employed. It had been during the earlier part of this voyage, before arrival at Old Sodbury's Island. Stephen had leaned far out of one of *Surprises'* stern windows, too far out, trying to net a creature in the luminescent wake, when he plunged overboard. Jack had gone into the dark sea after, under the misapprehension that the cutter was being towed behind *Surprise* and they could clap on. Instead, of course, they drifted in the sea until they were spotted by a frightful band of south sea female islanders, sailing their fore and aft out-rigger craft, a *pahi* as Cook had called them, with great alacrity, and pursuing cannibalism and the unsexing of men; Stephen shuddered as he recalled their gruesome 'trophy wall' with its' many exsiccated purse-like vestiges tacked to it, like so many prize fish. During their time on board, one of the younger women had spotted a shark in the water and, stripping herself mother naked without the slightest hesitation, she dove in after it, carrying a knife in her teeth and swimming like a dolphin, much in the way he had just seen the Sandwich Islanders do.

As Stephen and Lale mounted and began to ride back, Stephen remarked these remembrances to Lale's ever widening eyes, and as Lale listened he grew more excited, until his smile could no longer hold back a giddy laugh, and he said:

'Tepano, you are the amazing fellow to escape them. Oh, my!' Lale rolled his eyes and made exaggerated faces, but went on: 'We know of these women, they call them the Gelding Girls, though I have never before this known anyone who had actually seen them. You are quite the amazing fellow, Tepano!' he said, and laughed again.

At that moment Akoni and Kiristopa called out: '*Aroha*!' greetings from the hilltop, about two hundred yards above and south of the Indian burial mound. The two dogs appeared and ran down to greet Stephen and Lale.

'Akoni, can you guess who Tepano, our *aikáne* here, has met with?' Lale could not contain himself, and Akoni seemed to strain to make a creditable guess as Lale continued: 'I shall grant you a hint,' Lale held his hand below his waist and made a motion with his fingers like a pair of scissors, while grimacing wildly.

'*Wáhine hemo hua?*' asked Kiristopa with an awestruck expression on his face.

'Yes!' cried Lale, and, turning to Steven, 'This is what we *kanakas* call the Gelding Girls in our language.'

'We have heard about them,' said Akoni, But we thought it was like a…' he looked at Lale, '*lono waie…*'

'Like a "rumour,"' Lale supplied the English.

'I'm surprised you would have knowledge of such a thing at all,' said Stephen.

'Oh, Tepano, I told you, *kanakas* know all, see all.' At this all three of the islanders gave each other knowing, conspiratorial grins. 'After all,' Lale continued, 'the Earl of Sandwich has never been to the Islands, but *kanakas* know plenty about him.' At the mention of the Earl, Akoni and Kiristopa burst out laughing and covered their faces with their hands. 'All the news of the great men of the world finds its' way to us, skimming across the oceans to whisper it in our ears from the waves.'

'You don't say,' said Stephen.

'Did you know King George is mad?' asked Lale.

'That's a false rumour, I'm sure, but for the dear's sake, Lale, never say that in front of anyone else from the ship, especially Captain Aubrey.'

'Perhaps you would prefer to know that Bouneparte, though devoted to his wife, is a cuckold, and more than once, too.'

'If that's so, then I shall pray for Josephine that no one ever speaks of it in front of Napoleon. My goodness, Lale, is all the bruit abroad on your islands this kind of salacious tittle-tattle? What must you think of the other side of the world, then?'

Lale laughed and Akoni said: 'More than anything we mostly think they work too much.'

'Some, fair to say most, do. Some are very engaged in their pursuits, as I myself am with natural philosophy. But some, who are very wealthy, can afford sheer sloth as well.'

'Ha-ha! See? That's good!' said Lale. '*Kanakas* live both ways. That is, if one of us is rich we are all rich, you see? And no one works very much. But *kanakas* are almost never poor, unless all of us are poor. Then we all have to work again until we are rich.'

'Well,' said Stephen, It appears it affords you ample opportunity for idle gossip.'

Lale laughed again and said: 'We hear the gossip of the world when we're rich, and see some of it for ourselves when we are not, and must sail out across the world to earn our keep. I have many cousins who trap beaver in a place called Idaho, for the Hudson Bay Company, and a few more down in South America right now who are *vaqueros*, or *paniolos* as we call them, herding cattle. For myself, rich or poor, either way is fine, although right now I'd like to start getting a ship headed back home.'

The four men rode on, Akoni and Kiristopa chattering away ten to the dozen in their rhythmic, mellifluous tongue, while Lale occasionally provided English translations of certain terms or particularly trenchant phrases. Stephen's admirable spotted bay clopped along steadily, and though Stephen was not especially given to horsemanship, he appraised this one an outstanding steed, possessing a smooth gait, even on this terrain. In the afternoon light the islander's skin looked a golden colour, the late sun glinting off everything in a most pleasing way, giving it a sumptuous luster, and Stephen's very being felt infused with joy.

Arriving at the hide-house they were greeted by a *kanaka* youngster who asked if Stephen could come look at his brother, who was having trouble breathing. Inside crouched a little bronzed fellow on hands and knees by the hearth, he looked up at Stephen and politely smiled between his gasps, showing perfectly even, shiny white teeth, but in his eyes shown serious concern. Náenáe approached him with her tail curled down but wagging slightly, and touched his shoulder with her nose.

'This just began today, then, did it? After Lale and I left?' Stephen stood him up, holding his arms out as the boy gulped for air like a landed cod.

'Lale, do you have your clarionet here?'

'Tepano…? Yes, but…'

'Quickly, then, pray allow me to borrow the bell for a moment, would you, Lale?'

Lale fetched a sailcloth bag in which he kept his clarionet case. He opened it, unwrapped the bell, and handed it to Stephen who asked for silence and then placed the large end against the boy's chest, while he held his ear to the small end and listened at a variety of locations, left and right, up and down. He turned to Lale again, and handing him the bell asked:

'Have you any place nearby where leeches can be found?'

'No Tepano, there are never any at all to be found hereabout.'

'Have you still the chillum, then, and have you any more of that *cannibis*, my friend?'

'*Melekini*?' asked Lale, perplexed, handing it over.

Stephen picked up a small Indian blanket and placed it on top of the boy's and his own head. Then, lighting a straw from the fire he inhaled the smoke but only into his cheeks. He then blew a small steady stream of smoke toward the mouth and nose of the young *kanaka*, releasing it very slowly in his direction, while Lale absently assembled his clarionet and speechlessly watched with the others. Stephen took another puff, and repeated this procedure twice more until, to everyone's surprise but Stephen's, the boy at last seemed to be catching his breath a bit. Stephen lit another straw and said:

'I shall start this burning and then hand it to you. I'd like you to take a very, very little breath into your mouth, slowly inhale it, and then gently let it out. Do you understand all that?'

The boy looked at Lale who said:

'*Hanu i loko, hanu i waho*.'

He turned back to Stephen and nodded, then he took the chillum and did just as instructed. He exhaled, took two more breaths, and his symptoms went away to an extent even Stephen hadn't expected.

'I feel all better, Doctor Tepano, all better! You are *àno nui* doctor, an important, good doctor. Thank you very much, Doctor Tepano, thank you!'

'Well, you were having an asthma attack. Has that ever happened before this?'

'Only one other time, but not this bad.'

'And where was that, and how long ago?' asked Stephen.

'It was here, not long ago,' the boy tried to think of a way to tell Stephen, but he found it difficult thinking in English calendar terms, the confounding organization of sunrises and sunsets into a confusing collection of days and weeks, sennights and fortnights, months and years, and so on.

'It was on a Sunday…' he looked at Lale, 'Remember the hot day that Keo stood up on the back of a horse and rode past the hide-house into the surf, then jumped off funny, and everyone laughed all night about it? When was that?'

'That was about a month ago,' said Lale.

'You said it was warm that day,' continued Stephen, 'Did you have the *viento desierte* as well?'

Both Lale and the boy thought for a moment, then nodded yes.

'I believe,' said Stephen, 'that these balmy winds are not so comforting for everyone. Something carried on this wind has precipitated this attack, but clearly the vapour of hemp answered quite well, as it usually does in these cases.' He looked back at Lale and then the boy and said: 'While these off-shore winds continue you may perhaps suffer another bout. If so, give it a minute or two to abate of its' own, and if it does not, take one or two very slow puffs, as you did just now, and the asthma will go away to be sure.'

Stephen turned again to Lale, who was attaching the reed to his mouthpiece with several wraps of string, and asked:

'Can you spare a gramme or two, Lale?'

Lale lifted one shoulder and held out his hand: 'That goes without saying, Tepano.'

Then he lifted the clarionet to his lips and played a beautifully liquid chromatic scale across the entire range of the instrument twice, the lower register bubbling with a throaty verve and the upper tones in pinpoint pitch, piercing yet rounded, in the characteristic fashion of that instrument's unique harmonic timbre. With his next breath he slowly played through the opening passages to Bach's sonata in D minor, then snippets Stephen recognized immediately as being from Haydn and Mozart.

'You sound like a very accomplished player, Lale.'

'Oh, me?' Lale had only been doodling, but everyone around the hearth in the hide house had been listening along with Stephen, and their smiles of approval and Stephen's compliment overwhelmed him and caused him to smile and blush extremely.

'I just play some little things I like to hear. You are very kind. *Mohalo*, thank you, *aikáne*.' He held the horn to his chest and bowed in a supplicatory manner.

'Tell me, Lale, have you a small boat that you could pull over to *Surprise* this evening? I would very much like to have you join Captain Aubrey and myself, and I expect we will start tonight in about…' Stephen looked at his watch, having utterly lost track of time, 'Oh dear, about two hours or less. I had best be returning to the ship, post haste.'

'I'll go with you to the Embarcadero and ask Jack Ditler if I may use his little dory that he keeps by the beach. I would be most honoured to play in such distinguished company.'

As Stephen turned to take a step toward the door, there was a loud squeal from Keiki Hae who had been resting at Stephen's heels, and Stephen went sprawling toward the floor, but was caught at the last moment by Akoni and Kiristopa who placed him back on his feet and then mockingly scolded Keiki Hae, who sat panting and staring up at Stephen with pure adoration. Stephen looked back at her and smiled sheepishly, shook his head and said: '*Cave canem.*'

'I see you have acquired a companion,' said Jack, when Stephen entered the cabin with his 'cello, Keiki Hae close on his heels, having refused to leave him at the Embarcadero.

'Yes, and I hope you don't think me impertinent, Jack, but I also invited Lale to join us tonight on his clarionet. He is a very good player I believe, an impressive autodidact, and most congenial company.'

'And from what you tell me a man of many parts,' said Jack, 'When is he expected to arrive?'

Before Stephen could answer the marine sentry knocked on the cabin door, and Lale, hatless, clarionet in hand, was shown in.

'Hello again, Captain Aubrey, and if you please, may I offer my extreme compliments on *Surprise*. My, what a wonderful ship this is, and understand, I have been aboard a good many different boats before this.' Lale looked across at the grand curving sweep of the stern windows and stopped short: 'This is the most beautiful cabin I have ever seen on a vessel.

'I am so very happy to be aboard this evening, Captain, thank you for having me.'

'You are very welcome.' Jack smiled at Stephen, 'We're rather fond of the old barky ourselves; and please, you may call me Jack.'

'Thank you, Captain Jack.'

Jack laughed and Stephen asked: 'What would Jack's *kanaka* name be, Lale?'

'Jack would be: *Keaka*.'

'How wonderfully tuned is the Sandwich Islander's ear for the unintended sounds that English speakers make, without ourselves ever hearing them?'

Killick came in with some wine, and, carefully eyeing Lale laid the tray on the desk saying: 'Which I brought a third glass as you wish, Sir.'

'Thankee, Killick,' and raising his glass to Lale, Jack toasted: 'May all the unintended sounds I make tonight on my fiddle be good ones.'

Lale was able to stand behind Stephen and play from his sheet music, which was propped on the curious cabinet Stephen's wife,

Dianna Villiers had given him. They began with a selection from Mozart in F major. Commencing with a single note from Jack's bow, the other two instruments then plunging in to form the chord and flow into the piece. Lale's horn blended instantly with the strings, and he proved a superb musician in all respects; excellent timing, a quick study and an outstanding improviser, and projecting always a strong warm tone so complimentary to Stephen's 'cello and so assured in its' expression, that Stephen had insensibly transformed into a much better, more focused 'cellist. Indeed, a Boccherini 'cello piece he had merely competently played through countless times was tonight a moving musical experience, imbued with a freshness and a purposeful spontaneity it had never before possessed.

Jack, too, felt his play improve: left hand more taut, more precise in its' peregrinations, bow hand seamlessly gliding along with the notes like silken threads. Many of Lale's improvisations proved inspirational to Jack, in particular on a simple little Couperin piece that heretofore Jack had always considered old fashioned. Lale had placed the chart on the stand and without hesitation played it through from the start with an insouciant nonchalance, engaging Jack in a zesty and protracted *duels obligato*, each exchanging four measure passages *ad libitae*, one building upon the last, with many of Lale's musical turns becoming wondrous little complete compositions in miniature; sometimes simple and deeply satisfying, sometimes a complex zigzag of broad intervals beautifully woven together by the single final notes. On into the night they played, including a very modern and lengthy Mozart tetrology which they played in its' entirety, until almost six bells, when they shared a final glass, and Jack agreed to go back with Stephen and Lale in the morning to see the humourous trees.

Chapter Eight

It would be a beautifully clear morning, winds light and balmy, sun streaming down, horizon drawn with a straightedge. Outside the hide-house two youngsters were engaged with an India rubber ball, playing a game that looked to Jack remarkably similar to Eaton's Fives. Stephen was most anxious to reiterate yesterday's journey, and this time he had remembered to bring along his copy of Lind's *Cacti Taxonomy*. He had also brought a large sailcloth bag containing two small, stiff otter hides, a bit of tallow in a jar, and a sewing kit with some sail repairing odds and ends; he had an idea for these items which he hoped to put to test. However, when they went in the hide-house three Sandwich Islanders and an Indian boy were already there, patiently awaiting the doctor's arrival.

The Indian had a hernia and Stephen took him first. Later, while he was treating the three *kanakas*, nine more Indians arrived, all with hernias. Stephen suspected that the use of these mission Indians by the friars was something closely akin to slavery, an institution Stephen found singularly detestable. These, however, were not conscripted slaves, but voluntary servants, though clearly being driven rather hard and heavy by someone to have so many cases of herniated viscera in such a small population. And yet, it would seem that in their eyes and for their purposes this is preferable to their former lives as pagan Indians, wild and free, fending against the relatively benign elements in this sub-tropical region. Whatever their reasons, it defied easy presumption with what little Stephen knew of the specifics of the Indians' circumstances.

As Stephen performed his medical work and ruminated regarding the local Indians' situation, Lale was on the other side of the oven with yesterday's asthma victim, still fully recovered, and two other youngsters. Despite his long experience seeing blood in battle, Jack was secretly a bit squeamish regarding many medical procedures, so he walked across the room to where Lale was giving a lecture of sorts on *kanaka* navigation.

Lale opened a clutch of sticks about three feet long like a large Japanese fan, revealing a complex lattice structure of thin and thick sticks, set in differing directions, which composed a sort of grid upon which were fixed a number of small shells of various sizes and positions.

'I'm afraid you'll find this very old-fashioned, Captain Jack,' Lale smiled, 'but it's how we have always done it, so I still show the squeakers. I don't wish to bore you.'

'On the contrary, Lale, navigation is a particular study of mine, I teach the sextant and the logarithms myself to as many as can grasp it. And it's always good to master as many differing methods as possible, so that when one method don't answer, due to weather or whatnot, perhaps another will.

'Is that the world's largest set of Napier's bones you have there, Lale?'

'Ha-ha! No, but you are very close, Captain Jack. This is a map.'

This was a puzzle Jack thought he might solve, and after some time viewing it, Lale interjected:

'I'll give you a hint, it's a map of the world around our islands.'

'Well...the shells represent islands, do they not?'

'That's a good start,' said Lale, and, smiling at the youngsters, 'Do you see? A Captain must be a good student!'

'The sticks I'm not so sure about...the large ones could be a sort of prevailing wind or neat current chart, but then the small sticks confuse me. Do they mark time somehow?'

'No,' said Lale, who, along with his young charges, was visibly impressed by Jack's attempt. 'You are very close, but it is simpler than that, I'm afraid. We don't use logs or logarithms, and we don't have to worry about noon, the North Star, or the nutations of the Earth for that matter, but since the olden times the *kanakas* have found all the other specks of land out there by following these stick charts.' Lale smiled mischievously, 'Sometimes you find another island instead, Lono will lead you there perhaps, but it is how we have always found these islands. As you say, sometimes weather prevents navigation, and in this case that can be particularly true. You see, we employ this method in the evenings when the sea is calm. The large sticks are currents which you must learn to recognize from long experience following the stick chart at sea. The navigator sits at the extreme bow end of the boat, in a chair that hangs out over the water, and feels the waves and currents, including the waves that are bouncing off islands.'

'You can feel the water redounding off of islands like that?' Jack was incredulous.

'Oh, from the hundreds of leagues; the best navigators, on a good night, can go out to the bow and tell you the exact direction in which to sail to anywhere.'

Jack sat stupefied at this information, while the youngsters beamed proudly at Lale, who continued:

'These thin sticks show where waves reflect from islands, which the currents can sometimes bend, as you can see.'

'And what a capital thing of beauty it is, too,' Jack leaned closer, 'what are these tiny little shells, all in a row?'

'Those are certain large reefs that may appear, and these markings around the edge show the primary directions from which most large storms have come, which can sometimes confuse things a bit.'

'To say the least,' smiled Jack, 'I dare say I've never seen weather at sea like these last few months. I speak of contrary, disobliging weather, with all the normal winds and currents ahoo, or not there at all; becalmed or near it, or blowing like Satan's teapot.'

'Very difficult to beat south these days, or so I am told.'

'Exactly, Lale. Right now we should be fetching Cabo San Diego, not anchored in this San Diego. I've had more experience in the Atlantic, of course, where it seems things are more reliable somehow,'

'We have been hearing from passing ships that the southern waters were unusually warm along New Spain, and then cooler south of the isthmus.'

'And with so many heavy storms along the way, I don't doubt why the sea itself is at sixes, sevens and nines. But it don't signify, since otherwise we probably would never have come so far north, and I'd have missed your fine lesson in navigation, Lale.'

Lale had captured an outstanding mount for Jack, an enormous beautiful speckled blue stallion, with a chalk white blaze down his nose that matched his three sox. Once accustomed to the local style of tooled leather saddle, with its' *tapadero* stirrups and its' strange *perilla* pommel, Jack found the riding to be intensely pleasurable, and at one point he and the Sandwich Islanders let the horses have a go at it for a few furlongs of the El Camino Real, their thundering hooves beating to quarters along the dusty roadway, with Náenáe in hot pursuit. Lale, bareback and barefoot as ever, set the blistering pace on a quick paint with Jack not far behind, standing in the stirrups, knees to the withers, and smiling ear to ear. It was fine riding and he was savoring every thrilling moment, while in the back reaches of his mind it also prompted thoughts of England and Ashgrove Cottage, where he kept his own stable of horses.

Kieki Hae stayed behind on the trail with Stephen, who had no desire to race, and was instead dismounting occasionally to walk his horse and collect various beetles, one of which Kieki Hae had found for him with her nose, and he was just able to rescue it before it was eaten.

At length they arrived at the Rancho Soledad's south pasture where they watered the horses, and Lale persuaded Jack to take two bites of the mushrooms before their bitterness put him off, and he washed it down with a large gulp of water and a sour expression.

'By god, Stephen, did you eat some of these yesterday? I prefer the taste of shoe leather to it. Lale tells me they are mildly intoxicating, yes?'

'Very pleasantly so, too,' said Stephen, 'it's affect on the spirit is the reverse of its' flavour I assure you, a very alert awareness of one's sensibilities that magnifies the beauty in every blessed sight and sound. And they certainly are quite harmless in these small amounts; I never had the least untoward result,' and as he spoke it occurred to Stephen that last night he had not had so much as a passing thought about laudanum before retiring--and not through any sort of abnegation--and he had dreamt wonderfully strange dreams through the night.

Tying the horses to a scrub oak, Lale led the way past the burial mound, down and down into the arroyo again, past the cane break, through the deep crack in the sandstone boulder, across the bluff face, and down the slippery waterfall to the beach. The dogs had been unable to climb through the sandstone rock and had turned around, presumably to wait by the horses, but when the five men arrived at the top of the waterfall and looked down, there were Náenáe and Keiki Hae, looking up expectantly, smiling and wagging tongues and tails, and beaming with pride in their feat. Theirs were the only footprints on the entire beach.

Jack looked to the west; the day looked very different than yesterday. The warm offshore breeze that had commenced at dawn had blown every trace of fog and dust far, far out to sea, and made the air so lucid it would obviate a telescope. Along the horizon was a razor thin reddish-brown band dividing the cloudless blue sky and the very cheery blue Pacific. Looking out across its' corduroy surface regular sets of combers could be seen marching in all the way out to the far edge of the world, finally to break on the beach in regularity with a sizzling thump. The *kanakas* were as happy as hounds to the hunt, and they pointed to a spot just to the south where the waves were forming large glassine tubes that smoked and peeled as they ground their way to shore, dissolving at last to a thick soup of white foamy bubbles.

'Captain Jack, you will bathe with us, yes?' asked Lale as Kiristopa and Akoni smiled and nodded encouragement, 'Did you ever swim in the surf before this?'

Jack looked at the sea, 'Like this? No, I have not.'

'Tepano says you enjoy a swim, however, and I assure you, you will find this most rewarding today!'

Jack looked at Stephen.

'Were I a swimming man I should go myself, Jack, but as you know I possess a curious lack of buoyancy. Lale tells me there are no rocks, so I assume it's safe, at least for a strong swimmer such as yourself that is. Although you may want to learn the *kanaka* technique of swimming hand over hand, crawling along the top of the water.'

Jack turned around and the islanders were already thirty yards down the beach, Akoni swimming out with a riptide. Lale and Kiristopa were at the water's edge beckoning to him, telling him to doff his clothes except for his smalls, they having wrapped a kind of loin cloth around themselves.

Kiristopa grinned wide: 'We don't want the waves to succeed where the Gelding Girls failed.'

Akoni was already getting in position on the outside when Jack and the others waded out, and Jack observed their method closely. As the wash from a wave raised the water to neck level he began to swim, trying their style with little success at first, with each wave losing as much seaway as he had gained.

'Dive shallow, but swim under the waves and foam, Captain Jack. A bit farther out, when it gets deeper and the big waves come, just dive to the bottom and grip the sand as the wave goes over you.'

This advice answered wonderfully until Jack reached a certain point where every time he came up for air yet another wave was directly upon him and he would have to dive again and try not to get dragged back to shore as the breaker rolled over him in a powerful rush of bubbles that would often push Jack downward with irresistible force. These were waves of scale now, and manifestly larger and more abrim with energy than they had appeared from the beach.

Between dunkings Lale and Kiristopa continued to encourage

Jack, managing to remain nearby through the seeming chaos, and their utter sangfroid with even the largest of these waves was edifying to Jack. Akoni, of course, had raced out between sets, having an expert's knowledge of this beach break, but Jack and the *kanakas* were going straight up against a set of large incoming ocean rollers.

Kiristopa pointed to the left just past the shoulder of a wave, where the foaming surface was sucking over the lip and out toward sea: 'Do you see the river, flowing in the ocean?'

Jack nodded and smiled, and began imitating as best he could the island-style swimming technique as he headed straight for the rip current. The wave grew and Jack pulled harder and kicked faster until the wave had almost formed on top of him, but just before it broke they were all three swooped up and over as the wave swept past them, pelting them hard with spray from the offshore breeze. Just like that they were now out of the fray and it was just as quiescent as a chapel. The thunder of the surf a few feet behind them seemed distant now, with the sound of it bouncing all the way back from the bluff, and the air hung in motionless repose between the sets.

Jack treaded water and watched as the first set came in just to the south. While the swell height appeared to Jack to be a bit under one fathom, the faces of the waves from crest to trough were about double that, pounding the shore with ineluctable brute strength. Lale, whilst in the very jaws of one such monster, called out step-by-step direction to Jack in a voice as calm as if he were having tea in a elegant drawing room. With the next set all the *kanakas* encouraged Jack to try the one forming within their sight. Jack began to move a bit to his left—'Very good read of the wave, Captain Jack!' Lale had called out—and the wave began to swell to a crest, with the pocket just ahead of Jack. He began to swim as fast as ever he could toward shore as the wave lifted him—'Go left, Captain Jack!' cried Lale—and he tried to turn. He was quite vertical now, and despite furious stroking he was being pulled back into the wave; abruptly he was jerked back and sucked around the curl. At the apogee he seemed momentarily suspended in the stillness of the air, the only sound he heard was Kiristopa saying: 'Uh-oh,' and giggling. With that he was promptly slammed down face first into the churning turmoil and plunged so deep his hand felt the sandy bottom once as he tumbled head over heels, over and over, almost running completely out of air until he finally popped to the surface gasping, and facing the opposite direction as he had expected; and he was almost all the way back to the shallows again.

He turned to the Sandwich Islanders who were staring in his direction with blank expressions. When Jack smiled, unharmed, they all burst into a jag of funny high-pitched laughter before another, larger wave came through, which almost caught the islanders off guard and blasted Jack all the way back to the beach where he found he had drifted almost a quarter of a mile south along the shore from their entry point. Despite the ignoble result of his first attempt, Jack felt tremendously exhilarated and he stood for a moment with his back to the shore and watched the *kanakas* swoop down one wave upon the next, 'like barn swallows,' just as Stephen had said.

'Jack,' Stephen came wading up behind him, carrying the two small otter skins, 'Try these on, would you, Jack?' He held up the skins which he had fashioned into odd, asymmetrical shapes using Lale's cane knife. Each skin had four holes in it with a pair of ropes rove through them.

'Try them on what part of my body, Stephen? You confound me, my dear!' Jack laughed at his own joke, but he had been laughing at everything all day, since swallowing the mushrooms.

'It's an idea I've borrowed from that great philosopher of the world, Di Vinci. Come up on *terra firma* and I shall show them to you; they're meant as an aid to swimming.'

Jack and Stephen waded ashore and Jack examined the stiff hides, which were about two feet long and had been handily crafted, thanks to the keenness of Lale's blade, and a type of cinching slipknot Mowett had taught to Stephen.

'The shape is meant to mimic the feet of waterfowl, you see,

Jack? In this case I was thinking specifically of the Churchill geese which nest at Owens Pond in Essex each year, the fastest swimmers known among the stegenopods.'

'Yes, I'm sure, but...'

'Put your right foot in these two ropes, now, and cinch it thusly. Once in my academic days while doing some studies at the *Museo de Catalunya* I happened upon some drawings of Leonardo's, and one of them was this idea for improving swimming. Of course, his drawings call for flappers on both feet and hands, but I only had time for the feet. Here, now, put the other one on then...'

'I should hope these are better for swimming than they are for standing or walking...' Jack took one step and fell on the sand, laughing. He looked down at the contraptions on his feet:

'They're funny looking, but then, everything is rather funny looking to me today, and they are handsomely crafted little gewgaws however they may answer...' the two men smiled, 'Let's put them on closer to the water and I'll give them a proper sea trial.'

'Thank you, Jack. I know it's a mere gubbins, but I relish the opportunity to put a design of the great Leonardo to an apodictic test.'

'I warn you, in my most recent test I literally fell flat on my face, as you no doubt observed.'

Stephen laughed, looked out toward the line of combers relentlessly marching in and said: 'Well, the waves are a palimpsest, are they not, with each one washing away the last?'

Jack carried the flippers out waist deep and again put them on and cinched them very tightly. He got off his feet and began to paddle again into the surf. The flippers resistance to the water slowed his kicks, but with the very first thrust he could sense Stephen's contrivances working, pushing him along in the water in bursts with each kick. As the first wave of foam swept over him he dove under but continued to swim forward under water, surfacing right in the jaws of a breaking set wave. He took a quick deep breath, dove and swam again, and this time when he broke the surface he was just a few feet shy of the spot where the *kanakas* were lined up, and still another large wave arose between them and Jack dove and swam once more, this time popping out right in the line up, and labouring mightily for air.

'You are very good, Captain Jack,' said Lale, 'you took an outstanding hammering back there, ha-ha!'

All the Sandwich Islanders took a keen interest in the foot flappers, and they had Jack swim about demonstrating them for some time. Although he was sure he was swimming at a faster pace than ever before he had, he found to some chagrin that the *kanakas* could still out-swim him, and with no apparent great effort. Nonetheless, the improvement was tangible, and Jack was eager to give it another go.

The four swimmers waited speechlessly all in a row for the next incoming set, treading water and gently bobbing in the southwest swell. A large pelican's wingtips could just be seen over the small wave crests, flapping furiously. He flew north and came into full view about twenty yards away along the long, wide, sweeping face of an unbroken wave. He spread out his wings holding them less than an inch above the glassy surface, and glided on the updraft created as the offshore breeze, the *viento desierto*, gained force going up the concave surface of the water. Jack watched him glide all the way across the face, easily a cable's length, without once flapping his wings. At the north end of the wave he turned and rose about twenty feet off the water and flew south, very purposefully looking downward. Apparently spotting what he'd been looking for, he stalled momentarily in the sky, his entire body assuming a wedge-like shape, then he plunged very fast into the water with a splash, bringing up a corbina in his bill.

Entranced with the pelican, Jack didn't see the set forming in front of him until it was too late. He dove to the bottom just as the weight of the lip came to bear on him, and he popped out well behind the breaker. Twenty yards to the south, Akoni was dropping in on the next, much larger, set wave and Jack's position afforded him a view right into the barrel of the monster.

Trying to place himself at the apex of the shoulder, Akoni's furious stroking combined with the offshore breeze to throw a halo of spray into the air about him, creating ephemeral rainbows around him. He tried to swim down the face, but instead he was lifted and hurled some distance through the air, landing at first with his hands, chest, knees, and feet all so well positioned that he skipped once like a stone, then slid a short way, the huge lip almost overtaking him the whole time, before piercing through the wave's face using his left elbow and shoulder, and diving for the bottom as the ponderous great mound of water closed over him with a resounding thump.

As each successive wave in the set passed and broke behind him, Jack would be pelted in the back of his neck with the blowing spray from the lip. The offshore wind, though fairly light at the water's surface, became momentarily very brisk as it raced up the perfectly curved contour of incoming waves, and provided the plentiful rainbows and fine sport for pelicans.

Lale motioned Jack to swim over to him and then pointed south to the hills.

'Do you see the little tree at the peak of that hill?'

Jack nodded, and now Lale pointed east toward the blufftop.

'And you see the black rock embedded in the cliff?'

Jack saw the rectangular shaped section that was part of a layer of rock near the top and nodded again.

'You wish to be at least as far out as the tree to catch the big ones, and if you get even with the black rock and wait, a good wave will come to you soon,' Lale smiled and his big teeth flashed in the sun.

Jack waited at the prescribed intersection through a long torpid lull, the peaceful sea in utter contrast to itself now, between sets. Twenty yards in front of him a seal swam by looking straight north, pretending not to see Jack. Some languid minutes later, as a wave broke just behind Jack, a nine foot long grey dolphin leapt completely out, arced through the air not ten feet from Jack's astonished face, plunged noiselessly back in and sluiced down the slope of the back of the wave with a faint, rapid lapping sound as the water's glassy surface was simultaneously shot-through like grape by the offshore spray.

The next wave began to form and Jack began swimming for position as Lale and the *kanakas* could be heard hooting at him. He felt the water rise up beneath him and begin to thrust him forward, but he was too late and ended up perched right at the top of the lip's curl, cold spray in his eyes and the wave threatening to pull him over the falls again. He briefly looked up toward the beach and the view was like that of looking off the roof of a house. Arching backwards he was able to avoid another pounding ride to the beach.

Immediately he spun and swam for the very next set wave, taking long strokes in the crawling style of the Sandwich Islanders, and pushing ahead with Stephen's duck feet. This time the wave seemed to be almost guiding him toward the pocket, he could feel a current sucking him into the very heart of it, and he heard Lale shout:

'The wave is yours, Captain Jack!'

He continued to pull himself parallel to the breaker and he felt himself being lifted and impelled forward as spray stung his face. At that moment a bowl formed beneath Jack, who was now almost vertical in the water. He put his left arm out and placed his hand against the surface in front of him as he had seen the *kanakas* do. Instantly he dropped down the wave with the celerity of a racehorse, the spray almost blinding him as the comber folded and enclosed him. He brought his right hand forward to join the left and as he did he sped up considerably to be spit out of the wave's end in a puff of smoky spray. He heard the wild cheers of the *kanakas* before he was enveloped and tossed about like a stormsail again under the powerful surging foam.

'By God, that was absolutely capital!' He said as he sputtered to the surface, 'Positively capital! What Joy!' He turned and swam back out, 'I must do that again!'

Do it again he did, over and over, all afternoon, until finally, just as he was peering through the spray and dropping into another behemoth, his right calf began to cramp severely. He tried to relax it as completely as possible as it dragged along the wave face, but the muscle was knotting up like a cricket ball, so he stayed with the wave and rode it all the way into the beach, where he ended up crawling up on dry land while being mercilessly bashed by the shore pound the entire way, and laughing to the point of weeping at his chaotic predicament.

Lale waited and caught one more real beauty, rode it in, and stepped on dry land about the same time as Jack. Akoni and Kiristopa had come in from the surf about an hour previous, and were now cleaning a dozen medium-sized corbina they had caught by merely wading into the surf armed only with sharpened sticks of cane. Stephen had gathered some dried wood from the grove of humourous trees, and Lale got out his scrutineers glass to light the fire.

'Wherever did you get that unusual lens, Lale?' Jack, very sharp set, was hovering over the food preparers.

'I made it, actually. Jack Ditler had an old broken telescope which he gave to me. The objective was missing, but the subjective was a thick, ancient old single element type. I ground it down myself, of course, to make it more powerful; it's not much good for looking through, but a very good fire starter,' Lale held it up in the light for Jack to look through.

Yes, it's a bit more translucent than transparent. What are you grinding it with?'

'I use ash with pipe clay and a bit of sea water, and I lightly strop sail cloth over the lens as one would polish shoes or a brass door handle; one hundred strokes one way, then I rotate it ninety degrees and do another one hundred strokes the other way, then flip it over and do the same thing again and again.' Lale handed the glass to Jack.

'I'm very happy to tell you I have some Pomeranian superfine sludge that may be able to clear this lens, it usually answers most amazing for that purpose.

'That is very fine in you, Captain Jack. You know a great deal of lenses then?'

'Well, I'm no master or nestor, but my friends, the Herchells, back in England, certainly are.'

'You are a friend of Sir William then?' asked Lale.

Jack's eyes grew wide, 'Stephen said you were quite the man of the world, Lale, but how on Earth do you know of Sir William?'

'I acquire all the English books and other reading material that passing ships will give me, to practise my English. Last year the first mate of a Boston hide ship gave me a box full of old Naval Chronicles and papers to the Royal Society and the like. Very interesting to me, even if it was a bit out-dated, or hard to understand, I was very grateful they would throw such treasures away.'

The corbina were laid across the fire resting on palm fronds, and more fronds were used as serving plates. This method of cooking proved delicious and the fish were consumed in a tiny fraction of the time it had taken to prepare them. Stephen de-boned some of it for the dogs who ravenously attacked it, and then Keiki Hae barked repeatedly, demanding more, but by then there was no more to be had. Lale pulled a straw out of the fire and lit his chillum, then offered it to Jack.

'I think I was a midshipmen the last time I tried any of this, but since we've no wine...' and Jack inhaled slowly, then letting out the smoke said:

'Stephen, those swimming concoctions of yours are amazing; they're perfect for this kind of surf swimming. What joy, Stephen! What great joy it was out there. It is so much more than what it seems from the shore.'

'I fear my contraptions are also what led to your gastronemius cramps, though, Jack.'

Lale exhaled one of his 'Oahu puffs' and said: 'I must tell you to be sure to leave those here where the padres will never find them. If they should even suspect that one little otter hide is being smuggled onto your ships, why, they would demand your immediate departure, or worse, I'm sure. Here, have another,' he offered Jack the fresh packed chillum.

As Jack lit the chillum Náenáe walked over to him and licked him twice across the face, making man and dog smile back at one another.

'This whole afternoon has been like a wonderful dream, I might say, thanks to you, Stephen, and these clever coves here,' Jack nodded with a flourish of his hand toward the Sandwich Islanders.

'Captain Jack, you learn very fast,' said Kiristopa.

'Captain Jack did splendidly,' said Lale, and all three islanders nodded in agreement, Kiristopa saying:

'Sprendali, indeed!'

Jack leaned back on his elbows and smiled: 'I declare this whole day splendid; the riding, swimming, eating, and company, all of them, *splendid*,' Jack humourously exaggerated the pronunciation of the word, 'I cannot recall feeling so carefree since...well, since sometime long before this whole commission started.'

Náenáe licked Jack on the ear, and Lale said:

'This beach has *káháhá*; it surprises sometimes.'

'It is the great beach of the world, is it not?' Jack laughed a bit giddily, and turned to Stephen:

'I'm obliged to say that the last time I felt this comfortable and at home in the world I was probably at my leisure in the club back in London.'

'The Black's?' Asked Stephen, 'the Black's in Saint James' Street?'

'Yes, exactly; I feel as at home here as if this beach were Black's.'

Chapter Nine

On Sunday Don Onofre De Las Pulgas sent a very showy buggy to fetch Jack and Stephen for dinner. It was drawn by two white horses and was lushly upholstered in the same tooled leather of Luis Loco's fine saddles. With Keiki Hae following behind, the driver headed for *El Camino Real* and then rode the half an hour north to the Rancho Soledad, a rather hot and dry ride, this being the second straight day of *vientos desierte*.

Don Onofre's *villa* proved as showy as his buggy, with gardeners and servants milling about the spacious grounds and a compound of several small brown stucco structures surrounding a sprawling one-story brick and mud manor. Once inside the doorway, the air in the sumptuously furnished interior was cool and comfortable, a striking contrast with the out of doors.

Don Onofre, appearing the embodiment of the *gente de razon*, greeted them as effusively as ever he could have, and led them directly to the dining rectory where they were the last of the half dozen or so guests to arrive. All the men stood as Jack and Stephen entered the room and were introduced in the kind of regal formality they had come to expect in this country. The meal itself seemed, to Jack and Stephen at least, almost like something out of another world. A few of the side dishes such as *frijoles fritos* and the local succotash they had seen only once before this, days ago at the presidio, but the rest of the table was set with a dizzying variety of savory collations, none of which Jack or Stephen had ever before tasted, and the whole meal was topped with a salad of rose petals in a courant sauce that was ambrosia.

Don Onofre stood up as the wine was poured: 'May I propose a toast to our British *amigos* in our struggle against Napoleon.'

He sat back down and began to engage Stephen in a discussion of South American politics, asking several uncomfortable questions of surprising penetration, particularly regarding Chilé. Up until now Don Onofre had seemed merely a loquatious fop, a rodomontade. One that was clearly accustomed to receiving the utmost deference from his personal coterie, and one who still could not resist gross braggadocio at every chance. In fine, that had been Stephen's initial and ongoing measure of the man right up until this moment, but somehow this gasconading coxcomb, isolated at this frontier, had a thoroughgoing knowledge of what Stephen had thought to be some of England's most sensitive secrets. Stephen of course claimed no knowledge at all of the subject, tried in vain to subtly change it, and attempted in general to retreat behind his blue spectacles and deflect Las Pulgas piercing queries by meekly demurring:

'I'm a natural philosopher with no real grasp of politics, I'm afraid.'

Was it possible Don Onofre could be some sort of intelligence agent? And if so, had he somehow smoked that Stephen was a counterpart? 'Intelligence' in any sense was not something he would have particularly associated with Don Onofre, and now suddenly he was coming at it far too high, too high by half. Couched as idle speculations, his words nonetheless were a clear adumbration of an intimate knowledge regarding certain putatively secret diplomatic strategies and motives. Things Stephen himself was aware of only through sheer happenstance. Things a layman, especially one as remotely situated as Las Pulgas was here, should have no way of knowing. Things that were concealed, covert, conflicting, and compromising. Stephen maintained an expression of impenetrable stupidity until at last Don Onofre grew pococurante toward the subject himself and suggested showing Stephen some of the amenities about the estate.

'I've several fine things that were brought here from very far away, some things that are most rare hereabout. I think it may surprise you to see some of these things here in California.'

Jack, seated at the opposite end of the table and engaged in another conversation entirely, had not been paying attention to the discursive Don Onofre's political colloquy, nor had he paid much attention to his own conversation, as he had been extremely distracted all through dinner by the touch of Doña-Fior's foot, periodically pressed gently, but deliberately against his own under the table. When her husband left the room with Stephen she grew somewhat bolder, giving Jack a meaningful expression.

Doña-Fior was, by any measure, an extraordinarily beautiful woman, and this evening she was in high looks; she was in very high looks. Jack noted she had the delicate scatlings of a Spanish xebec, but she was rigged like a ship-of-the-line. From the brief glances he stole, it appeared to Jack she was nearly the apotheosis of female form, the cynosure of this room, and no doubt any other she should occupy. Not at all fair, her skin was instead of a glowing golden colour, and her deeply translucent green eyes and bright white teeth sparkled against it like diamonds whenever she spoke or smiled. Jack had been discussing the excellent riding available here with two of the other guests, trying to avoid eye contact, but now she said to him:

'We don't use those that run the hills, but we have our own horses here at the rancho.' She stood up, and so did Jack and the other men at the table, 'I would be most happy to show you the horses in our *caballeriza* right now if you wish. We have some very pretty ones, for the riding as well as the draughting.'

In the interregnum, Don Onofre's tour was proving every bit as surprising as reported, and of course he was not the least backward in boasting of it all. His manor, or *villa*, situated as it was in this ultramarine dominion, nevertheless appeared to have every imaginable luxury that Don Onofre could conceive, including a large collection of foils and a courtyard devoted to fencing practise, a superbly appointed music room that featured both a beautiful harpsichord (with the normal black and white keys reversed in their colours) as well as an eighty-five key piano-forte from Italy that Don Onofre claimed had once belonged to the great Italian Maestro Marco Pietri.

At length they reached the very up-to-date billiard parlour with a table of the most current English type, four pockets going around the corners and two at the sides; and, as Don Onofre was quick to point out, this was no pinchbeck, but a genuine Thurston and Company table, with a Simonis baize topping for the green. Stephen absently ran his hand across the table, 'I've relatives in Merino who sold wool to the Simonis family...'

Stephen bit his tongue; he was instantly peeved with himself over this revelation, however insignificant it may have been. He had spoken thoughtlessly, there was no call for it, and it was very much out of Stephen's character to blather, especially about himself, since the less known the better for everyone. And he had let his guard slip with Las Pulgas, for all love, and of all people, since he still wasn't sure if the Don was a fox or a fool. With the exception of his brief but uncanny conjectures regarding Chiléan and English relations he had otherwise never veered from his usual preening prattling self, and Stephen could only hope that that persona was not a facile posture.

'Excuse me, Doctor, I did not hear you.'

'I was just admiring the billiard cloth.'

'Do you play, Doctor?' Don Onofre walked over to a wall-mounted rack that held a couple of ancient looking maces and a few of the newer straight type of cues. He took down two fine white ash sticks with ivory ferrules at their working ends. Don Onofre pointed to them:

'I used to have these jeffrey-cut, but as you can see they are now tipped with a piece of roughened bridle leather; it is the very latest thing.'

Stephen wished to beg off, but Don Onofre had already laid the cues down and begun lighting the many candles in a wrought-iron framework hung over the table. As the room illuminated Stephen could see that in all respects this was the most thoroughly equipped billiard parlour he had ever been in, public house or private. On the wall over the mace and cue rack was a shelf holding a Thurston and Company scoring marker, with its' two clock-like faces numbered one to twenty, as well as a brass scale for assuring the weights of the balls balanced. The candelabra's frame matched that of the table, with eighteen candles mounted in three rows, two along the table's sides and one down the middle, creating a luminent annulus over the area of play. Just outside the glow were two high wooden benches, flanking the room. On the table were now three ivory balls, two white and one red, and all perfectly matched in size.

Don Onofre had wholly laid aside the use of the mace, along with the port and king, in favour of the most current styles of play. He turned to Stephen and asked:

'Do you know the game called *carambole*?'

'I know the little red Spanish fruit,' Stephen replied impertinently.

Las Pulgas laughed and pointed to the red ball, 'That is the *carambole* in this game, and you must put the little fruit in a pocket by striking it with your cue ball,' he pointed to the white ball at the near end of the table.

'I see,' said Stephen.

'You may also pocket my cue ball for points, but first, if possible, you wish to "*carambole*."'

'...To play a cannon in other words?' asked Stephen.

'Exactly,' Las Pulgas smiled, 'You do play I see. If you *carambole* first, you then receive more points on any balls you subsequently sink. Games can sometimes be over very quickly, which is perhaps why it is favoured among bettors.'

'It sounds,' said Stephen, 'like a version of the French game, "Hazards."'

'Just so,' said Las Pulgas, dabbing some white chalk on the leather tip, 'Here, let me show you a fancy shot I have learned before we begin.'

Placing his cue ball in the middle of the table and the other two balls near the side pockets, he leaned over the table and laid his left hand flat in front of his cue ball with his fingers spread. Holding his thumb against his hand he rested the cue in the groove between his thumb and forefinger, where it could slide in an easy, smooth motion. He took a few practise strokes, and Stephen noted that he intended to strike the cue ball beneath its center point, just above the table, perhaps to make the ball jump, Stephen guessed. Instead when the ball was struck it rolled into the first ball and knocked it into the pocket, but then the cue ball bounded off the object ball and began to roll backward all the way across the table, hazarding the other ball as well.

'Do you see?' Don Onofre pointed to the leather tip, it is like witchcraft, no?'

No, it is not, thought Stephen, but it is a beautiful demonstration of the laws of matter. The effect of Las Pugas' chalked leather tip on the ball had been distinct, the cue ball fairly leaping backward on impact. Stephen had heard of the use of so-called 'side-stroke' or 'English' to influence the movement of the balls, but this was the first such clear a demonstration of it as he had seen, and Stephen instantly grasped it. Like everything brilliant, it was simple; by increasing the coefficient of friction between the striking tip and the ball a great deal of spin could be imparted to the cue ball that was irrespective of the direction the ball was traveling. When it struck the other ball it stopped its' motion in that direction, and the contrary spin could now cause the cue ball to roll 'backward.'

'That one would be two points for the cannon, plus three points for sinking the red ball, and two points for hazarding your ball, ha-ha!'

'May I knock a ball or two about, just to get thc feel of it? I've always used a mace before this.'

Stephen leaned over the table, with his left hand and two feet forming an equilateral triangle, and rested the cue along his hand as he had seen Don Onofre do. He placed his right eye just above the cue shaft and stroked the ball. It rolled down the table to the rail and bounced back with surprising energy.

'I have eighteen strips of flannel layered in the cushions,' bragged Las Pulgas, 'They rebound well, yes? And you will find their bounce is perfectly true, or at least almost perfect. In that respect the leather tip has had an uncertain influence on the trueness of the redound, I find.'

Las Pulgas then went on to expound at some length regarding his nebulous billiard theories, while Stephen utterly ignored him and tried out several simple shots to observe the behaviour of the balls. In general he found that instead of the jerky thrusting sort of poke that Las Pulgas had employed in his demonstration, a slower, smooth stroke, through the ball, allowed it to acquire the more spin. And not just the cue ball spun; when Stephen applied side-stroke to the cue ball it imperceptibly transmitted a portion of that spin, but in the reverse direction, to the object ball. Stephen could tell this because if that ball then struck a cushion the spin could greatly change the angle of reflection. After a few minutes of this experimentation, Stephen decided that this style of play was better suited to him, and that Las Pulgas, although he owned this magnificent billiard equipment, had some fundamental misunderstandings about its use. Stephen had always lacked skill with a mace, and in fact, rarely played billiards at all, but he was immediately adapting his shot-making to the straight cue stick, since in its way it was more like aiming a fowling piece, something at which Stephen was already adept; indeed, few on board *Surprise* knew that Doctor Maturin was perhaps the best marksman among them. They were equally unaware of his extensive victorious experience in sword dueling, which in some respects of its action also compared to the handling and thrusting of the cue.

Stephen continued moving about the table, refining his practise by methodically testing spins at various angles and observing his cue ball. In short order he found he could easily increase or decrease the length of roll, as well as the angle of carom, although it required considerable focus. Having once selected where to strike the cue ball Stephen aimed right down the stick, through the cue ball, and softly stroked directly at the target. Don Onofre was midway through a detailed remembrance of the way in which the table had been brought from Boston, and all the way 'round the Horn, aboard the *Pilgrim*, when Stephen stood up and said:

'Would you care to lay an amicable wager, Don Onofre?'

As they rode back together to the embarcadero that evening both Jack and Stephen were unusually terse with each other, but neither noticed the other's breviloquence, as they were both self-absorbed at the moment, each with their own particular worry and regret. Stephen had dreaded this visit to Rancho Soledad in the first instance, perceiving Las Pulgas to be petty, vain, and repellent. Jack, on the other hand, had looked forward to it greatly, as he had every aspect of this heretofore wonderfully relaxed respite in San Diego; perhaps too relaxed. Now, in this sudden, unwelcome reversal of fortune, everything seemed to be going precipitously wrong.

Stephen's main intent in challenging Don Onofre had been to shut him up. Unfortunately, Don Onofre proved an uncommonly good billiards player, and more boorish than ever in victory, doubling his boasting during his own innings, and spouting pedantic advice to Stephen all during his, all the while lightening Stephen's pocketbook by ten pounds. Playing the fool to Las Pulgas in a gaming room was not something Stephen enjoyed, but what was really disturbing his peace of mind was still Don Onofre's informed discussion of Chilé, which Stephen continued to turn over and over in his mind. If he really was aware of these things, how? He seemed possessed of just enough detail that it could hardly be guesswork, but what other way to explain it? And that was the chafe; if Las Pulgas was an intelligence agent, he was one with a strange notion of discretion. His behaviour was the reverse of normal, he appeared to be openly, even casually, sharing every bit of information in his possession on the subject. So it was still impossible for Stephen to determine if Don Onofre was the utter ass he appeared, or an artful, and very clever cove. Whichever the case, he would have to make that determination on his own, as he obviously could not discuss any of this with anyone, even Jack.

Jack was of course also keeping his own counsel, primarily excogitating the numerous extenuating factors that might serve to mitigate his own culpability. To be sure, from the start Doña-Fior had been extremely forward, and Jack knew he had done nothing to prompt her behaviour; indeed, was very surprised by it. After they had all left the table together she had blithely contrived to separate Jack from the other guests, getting him alone in the stable; that had most certainly not been any of Jack's doing. And when he smoked what was afoot he did, in fact, turn to walk out, and offered her through the door like a perfect gentleman. But he is a gentleman who has been at sea and far from home for a very long time. Doña-Fior had stepped forward but then shut the door and blocked it, spinning around to face Jack, she had already hastily opened the bodice of her dress. Indelicate conduct with Don Onofre's wife was absolutely something Jack did not wish to engage in, under any circumstances, and yet there was Doña-Fior standing before him, whispering seductively, and touching him intimately...

So they both rode in silence, Jack calculating what might be the earliest practicable tide to ship out of this port, and Stephen still puzzling Las Pulgas' words. Neither of them were now taking notice of the wondrous palette of crepuscular desert colours slowly fading into the gloaming, as the two white horses cantered along *El Camino Real* at a syncopated gait, and Kieki Hae criss-crossed the path before them in the mistaken notion that she was herding the two horses home.

At the embarcadero there was news that Luis Loco was back, and there was also a message from Bonden for Captain Aubrey, asking if he would have Jack Ditler take him directly to *Enderby* at his earliest convenience.

'I'd be happy to come back and take the doctor over to *Surprise* afterward, if you like,' said Jack Ditler, 'I'll make it my last run of the day.'

'I hope you don't mind, Stephen,' Jack gazed out toward the anchored ships and then back to Stephen.

'On the contrary,' Stephen looked at Jack Ditler, 'I believe I'll have time, will I not, to walk over to the hide houses with Kieki Hae and look in on my asthma patient?' It was just as well, too, thought Stephen, because his mind was far too overwrought for music tonight, and now he would not have to beg off with some clumsy explanation; and he hoped that perhaps a few moments in the presence of the *kanakas* would serve to invaginate his unhappy mood. But that was not to be fate's plan.

Jack was unaccustomed to ever seeing such a serious expression on Bonden's face as he saw now, upon arrival aboard *Enderby*. They walked together to the quarterdeck and Bonden said:

'It's the *Hermiones*, Sir, there was more trouble with some of them this afternoon.'

'Pray, what sort of trouble, Barrett?'

'Two of them capped it, Sir, and which I'm obliged to add the first of them died at my hand, sad to say. I never intended it, Sir, but there it is.'

'I'm certain you didn't. What exactly happened?'

'How it got started I can't say, But a bit before three bells in the noon watch I was told by old Tanzi that there was some commotion down in the mutineer's brig, so I made all haste to see what it was about. By the time I got to the hold there were three marine sentries already there, holding their muskets on the mob, which had quieted down.'

'But the two that capped it?'

'Yes, Sir, I'm getting to that. It seems that at the change of noon watch one of these *Hermiones*, a Patrick Harris, started demanding to see you. They calmed him down, but then when I got there, another of them got it in his head that I was you.'

''He took you for me?' asked Jack.

'Yes, Sir, and he attacked me.'

'He attacked you viciously just because he thought you were Jack Aubrey?' Jack was trying to be light-hearted, but Bonden was having none of it.

'Well, Sir, He went after me with a nail, a great large fellow he was too, name of Bottenhorn. He seemed to have gone mad, and to defend myself I cuffed him as solidly as ever I could on the side of his head; I was merely trying to knock the man down.'

'And did you?' Jack knew the probable answer to his own question, since he knew Bonden to be a one-time boxing champion in the Navy's inter-mural pugilistic contests.

'Yes , Sir, I did that, but I'm afraid he struck his head on something when he fell, and the blow killed him, Sir. Then all the rest of them turned 'round to me, and this Patrick Harris fellow started at me with blood in his eyes. What happened then was most unfortunate, Sir, but one of the sentries, the youngest of the marines, Mr. Teesley, screamed at him to halt--'

'And did he then stop?'

'No, Sir, he didn't, but one of the other prisoners, Mr. Muspratt, had at that moment grabbed him by the left shoulder and tried to turn him around, I heard him start to caution Harris of what he was about when the musket went off behind me and Muspratt fell dead.'

'What did the other prisoners do at that point?'

'They was shocked, Sir, as were we all, just dumb-struck. If I may speak free, Sir, they must know they're all to be hanged in the end anyway, but Muspratt was the oldest of them, and maybe the best man out of the whole sad lot of them. I had spoken to him myself on occasion as he acted as a sort of diplomat for the rest of the *Hermiones*. He once told me himself that he and many of the rest had had nothing whatsoever to do with the mutiny, but they'll all hang just the same, and there's nothing to be done for it.'

'Just so,' Jack looked out over the taffrail, 'Where are the bodies?'

'We put them in the orlop for now, to see how you wished to handle it.'

'Good,' Jack took his eyes off the horizon, narrowed them slightly and looked at Bonden.

'How's our watering going, Barrett?'

'We're still at it,Sir.'

'Yes, but how soon do you suppose that we could get adequate water aboard for both vessels?'

'Which, if that's all we wanted to do, Sir, we could probably be done by tomorrow evening.'

'Excellent! Make every effort to do just that. First thing in the morning send someone to the mission to fetch Fat-Arse Jenks and whatever other *Surprises* or *Enderbys* that are there working on the aqueduct. And, make something up if necessary—don't tell them we're cutting our stay short here—but put out the order that I want every man ashore to be back aboard before two bells in the second dog watch tomorrow evening.'

'May I ask when, exactly, you expect to weigh, Sir?'

'I hope the day after tomorrow, before dawn, when slackwater should occur about an hour before first light. If the offshore wind holds up that long we can slip out between two days, so to speak, take a broad reach, and get a fast jump on our journey south.'

Jack looked past Bonden and saw Tanzi and Nic Crofter standing just off the starboard quarterdeck.

'Captain Aubrey, permission to board the quarterdeck and have a word, Sir?' Tanzi was still wearing the sailcloth eye patch that

Stephen had fashioned for him.

'Yes, of course, Tanzi, I'm very happy to see you again, and you also, Mister Crofter; you seem to have grown a bit since we left Old Sodbury's Island, haven't you?'

'It were young Nic here who found it all and got suspicious of it in the first place,' said Tanzi, 'and it's his clever theory to explain it, not mine, Sir.'

'Whatever are we speaking about, Tanzi?'

'I think it best we show it to you, Sir.'

They led Jack over to the starboard chains and Tanzi said:

'We was moving some empty casks for the watering and Nic noticed this and hauled it in.'

Coiled in a puddle on the deck was a sixty fathom length of rope with an old magnum port bottle tied to it.

'It's got about a half pint of fresh water in it.'

Jack looked at it, and turning to Nic asked:

'So, what do you make of it?'

'Well, Sir, nothing at first, but then Tanzi uncovered this when we moved a barrel,' Nic picked up a sailcloth bag that held an olive jar, with a few olives still left in it.

Jack raised a brow, 'Some sort of stowaway?'

Tanzi nodded at Nic and pushed the air in front of him with his hands, 'You go on, *bach*, you tell the Captain what you think.'

'Well, Sir,' Nic began slowly, 'not a stowaway exactly as you might say, in the everyday sense.' He looked over at Tanzi and then back to Jack, 'It's just that I was close; me and Tanzi was both of us quite close—why, he dropped a marlin spike that almost crowned me—that is we were close by when the Hermione was shot from the foreyard.'

Jack looked again at the line and the bottle, 'Yes, pray, continue, Nic.'

'Well, Sir, which it was a miracle that he was hit like that, in one shot; you could hardly see at all, it was only just first light. Westerdale told me himself he thought he'd missed until he saw, with all the rest of us on deck, the man fall into the water with some kind of a gut wound.'

'You don't think he was killed then?' asked Jack.

'I'm not sure he was even really shot. I asked myself: why would he have leaped, as he must have, to avoid landing on deck?' We wasn't listing enough at the time for him to just *fall* overboard from the foretop, so he must have jumped, at least a bit. And then I wondered why he would have climbed up there to begin with?'

'So you think this Jonas fellow could have swum under *Enderby* to get to this line hanging off the mizzen starboard before the ship passed him by?'

'We were making very little headway and, yes, I do think it's a feat that a swimming man could do, particularly one sailing to his own hanging.'

Far-fetched as it seemed, Jack had to admit it made a certain amount of sense. Westerdale's shot had seemed extraordinarily good practise, and why he fell to the sea instead of the deck had been a question Jack had briefly asked himself at the time, and then forgotten about. Jack tried to remember how long a time had passed between the shooting and their making port here: three days. If this man did survive the musket, was it only to perish at sea? Or could he be…

Jack's mind froze with horror as he suddenly remembered Lale saying on the afternoon when they first disembarked that a sailor from one of the ships had already been seen ashore just before them. Jack had dismissed it as a mistaken notion at the time, but now, knowing Lale to be the straight-ahead fellow that he was, it seemed a disturbing possibility that in fact this *Hermione* mutineer may have actually managed to escape into New Spain. Jack turned to Nic:

'Have you shown these things to anyone else, or told them about your ideas?'

'No, Sir, just Tanzi here.'

'Good. Pray, please keep it that way, and you, too, Tanzi.'

Tanzi nodded: ''Aye, Sir, goes without saying, Sir.'

Jack smiled at Nic, 'You're on your way to being a first-rater, young man, thank you very much for bringing this to my attention,' he turned to Tanzi, 'and you also, Tanzi. Very good initiative, good sailoring; but I repeat, gentlemen, this matter is of the strictest naval confidence, and should never be spoken of again, unless I specifically tell each of you otherwise, understood?'

Tanzi and Nic silently nodded, which Jack thought to be the most satisfactory answer possible. Jack's boat was ready to pull him over to *Surprise* for the night, so with that he bid them good evening.

As Stephen was approaching the hide house he saw Lale engaged in a conversation with one of the local Indians. The Indian appeared to be doing all the talking along with a great deal of vigorous gesturing. Kieki Hae ran ahead and was greeted by a furiously wagging Náenáe. As Stephen got closer he could hear the Indian, who was speaking in the coarsest Spanish dialect Stephen had ever heard, proclaiming that Lale and everyone else on the beach owed him money. He then became reconciliatory, offering that if he had been Lale and the others perhaps he may have acted the same. In the very next breath he was again condemning anyone aship or ashore, and as Stephen joined them the Indian turned to him, angrily asking:

'*¿Y, usted?*'

'Pay him no mind, Doctor, he is crazy. That's why they call him Luis Loco. He's upset that some of his saddles were used while he was away, and he wasn't paid, that is all, pay him no mind.'

But Luis Loco abruptly dropped the whole subject himself, and instead started teasing Kieki Hae who had taken a keen interest in a piece of parchment writing paper that happened to be hanging out of Luis Loco's pocket. He took it out of his pocket and held it up over his head, bobbing it in her direction a couple of times. She wagged her tail purposefully and looked up, first at the prize, and then at the laughing Luis Loco. Suddenly she leapt straight up, pushing off Luis' chest with her forepaws, to an improbable height well above his head, where she snatched the paper with a flourish and then trotted off with it, Náenáe following close behind. Luis screamed at her in his rude Spanish, but she wasn't listening and ran to the other side of the hide house.

After a good deal more grumbling Luis Loco finally wandered off towards the hills, and Stephen and Lale went into the hide house where they found Akoni, Kiristopa, and Lopaka squatting around the hearth, chattering away in their rhythmic tongue, punctuated by equal amounts of cackling laughter. When they saw Stephen they all greeted him with '*Aroha'* and then switched to English.

'You needn't speak English on my account,' said Stephen, 'I enjoy listening to the sound of the Sandwich Islander's speech, and I try to extract what meaning I can from some words Lale has taught to me.'

Kiristopa pointed to Akoni and said: 'He's the one you should listen to, He's had more practise at talking than anyone,' and all the *kanakas*, including Akoni, burst out laughing again.

Stephen had only a few moments before he would have to return to the embarcadero to meet Jack Ditler, but he sat for a moment and allowed his thoughts to repose among the dulcifying foreign words, and his present, pleasant companions. How much more free of vexation, thought Stephen, and how much more robust and rich a world they live in, where no one has either worry or wealth unless it be shared by all. How long could their arcadian *modus vivendi* endure, wondered Stephen, now that the procrustean world had found them. He recalled an ironical story he had once heard about Sir Joseph Banks pressing flowers from Otaheite in a copy of Milton's *Paradise Lost*.

Stephen's thoughts were interrupted as Náenáe trotted into the hide house with the parchment paper Kieki Hae had stolen from Luis Loco, now clapped in her mouth. She laid the paper on the ground in front of Stephen and sat panting, smiling at him. He looked down at it, and what he saw shocked him as nothing ever had before. There, crumpled on the ground in tatters before him, torn and dingy as ever it could be, was a draught, counterfoil still attached, signed by no less than the clerk of the King of England, George the Third

Himself, and made in the amount of six hundred and seventy-five thousand pounds sterling.

Náenáe, sensing Steven's great distress, put her head down and her tail between her legs, and eyed Stephen warily. He snatched up the horrid thing and stuffed it in his pocket and tried to regain his composure. He had recognized it right away, of course, it was one of twelve such notes contained in that loathsome fretful box they had received from *Danae*. There had also been three cover letters of the most confidential nature; three very different and conflicting cover letters that were never meant to all three be read together, since each was intended for a different possible recipient, depending upon who held the reins in Chilé, and what expedient was therefore held to be in Britain's best interests. It seemed evident Las Pulgas had read all three, but it wasn't clear he actually grasped the authenticity and import of the documents, and it also seemed unlikely he had knowledge of the money, for he hadn't mentioned it at all, and he was quite incapable of keeping such a secret. It seemed more probable to Stephen that he mistook them for some sort of political pamphlets, and had brought their subjects up to Stephen only to impress him with how up-to-date was his knowledge of the world. So--*Sancta Simplicitas*!--Las Pulgas was not a spy; that was no longer an issue. But would that it were, thought Stephen. That anxiety had been blissful compared with this outcome; perhaps Las Pulgas still had the letters, perhaps not, but somewhere out there were eleven more of those dreadful notes drawn on the Crown, and, unimaginable as it may be, somehow this Luis Loco character had obtained at least one of them. Náenáe was still looking straight into Stephen's eyes, panting and now again smiling. Stephen looked at her, rubbed her behind her ears, and then stood up to return to *Surprise*.

'Lale, I should like to speak to Luis Loco first thing in the morning if that's possible. Do you know how I may contact him?'

Whether or not Lale could sense Stephen's suddenly disarranged state of mind he gave no hint, but he assured Stephen he could easily fetch Luis in the morning, and Stephen was grateful that Lale had expressed no curiosity regarding his inquiry.

'I'm glad to find you here, Jack,' said Stephen as he entered the great cabin, 'I must speak with you,' he gave a sober look, 'privately.'

'Yes?' said Jack, with uncharacteristic timidness.

'We may be dished, brother,' Stephen blinked his pale blue eyes.

'Well,' said Jack softly, 'I plan to weigh as soon as possible, before there's any trouble about it.'

Stephen went on with a slightly puzzled look, 'There's already trouble aplenty, Jack, that's what I'm telling you, and I say we can't leave until we resolve this.'

Now it was Jack's turn to look puzzled, 'Resolve it how?'

'By gaining return of the items, of course, and how did you smoke it?'

'Return? Stephen, what are we talking about here?'

'That accursed box from *Danae*, how did you take my meaning?'

'Oh, the box,' said Jack smiling, 'not to worry about that, it's in a very safe place.'

'I don't think it is, Jack, look at this,' Stephen withdrew the draught from his pocket and laid it on the great desk.

Jack stared at the bill for a moment and said: 'A clever forgery, Stephen, nothing more, I assure you. The box is safe, I'm sure of it; but where did you find this?'

'Jack, listen to me, during dinner Don Onofre made several comments that disturbed me greatly in their recondite knowledge of British secrets. I believe he has read the cover letters and that the other eleven notes are still to be recovered.'

'Well then, let me just put this little concern of yours to rest, Stephen,' Jack reached into the footwell of the desk and found the short butt. Stephen locked the cabin door from the inside and Jack pulled the box out of its cubby and placed it on the desk. 'There, you see, Stephen, there's your box, safe and sound.'

'My sealing wax has been broken.'

'Perhaps it was jostled, with all these many miles at sea,' and Jack twisted the clasp, popping it open.

He looked into the box, then at Stephen, and then back at the box again.

'Red Hell and death!' He stuck his hand all the way in and felt the empty bottom: Empty as Pandora's Box--no, worse than that--for Pandora's Box had at least still contained Hope. But hope, if there were any to be found, certainly did not reside now in this despicable box.

Chapter Ten

The noon sun was absolutely blinding as it reflected off the flinty dirt roads and the squat mud and stucco buildings of San Diego Town. But inside the small adobe cantina, with its' thick walls, it was dark, cool, and quiet as evening, except at the windows and doorway, where shafts of bright, hot, yellow light pierced through to the interior like glistening golden shafts. The bartender, who also took care of the dry goods crib next door, was alone inside save for one other man, a very large hulking English sailor sitting in the back shadows, his face out of sight in the blackness. He had been sitting in that same spot for the most part of the last three days drinking, but very little, and not spending the kind of money the bartender had expected from so corpulent a sailor. In fact, the *Ingles marinaros* had thus far been a general disappointment to the barkeep since most of them didn't even know of the cantina's existence or location. Unbeknownst to the bartender was the fact that only one of the *Enderby's* spoke any Spanish at all, and that one had ill-advised his shipmates that when ashore they should ask:

'¿Donde esta la villa publica?' ('Where is the public house?')

Unfortunately, most of the locals thus queried assumed they were being asked for the whereabouts of a whorehouse, and most took some considerable umbrage at the question itself. If they answered at all it was to say, with righteous indignation, that there was no such place. Only one man, a Spaniard who had been to London, had understood the question properly, but he had no English, and his directions to the cantina were incomprehensible to anyone who didn't speak fluent Spanish. Except for this fat sailor in the corner the only other Englishman to find the place had been brought there by Luis Loco the morning the English ships arrived, and he had been of the opposite type; a callow, half-drown looking wretch, who nonetheless was a copious consumer in his brief visit to the cantina. The barman smiled to himself remembering the outrageous counterfeit check he had produced, asking if he could trade it for some trail provisions, apparently unaware of the putative value of it, since he admitted he could not read it himself, but just thought it looked important. The Englishman's brash conceit so amused the barman that he agreed to the bargain, but only if the sailor would also hand over the additional ten shillings in his pocket; the ten shillings Patty Harris had given him. For that, he ate and drank enough to be two such men as the fat man now in the corner, and then he left with a water can, a pot, a small knife, two blankets, a poncho, a shirt and a pair of breeches, some tortillas, beans, rice, and ten pounds of pork salt. He was also offered some of the excellent local olives, but declined them with the cryptic aside that his constitution could no longer abide them. He packed all of it onto a horse Luis Loco had caught for him, and the two of them had headed off for the *Rancho Sepùlveda*, two days ride to the north. The barkeep had heard that Luis had come back yesterday, but thus far he had not made his appearance at the cantina, which meant it would be another slow day, with no *Ingles marinaros*. Unfortunately, with Luis departing the day the ships arrived, there had been no one to guide the Englishmen all the way to this tiny, non-descript, mud hut which didn't so much as display a sign or have a shingle hung to signify that it was even a place of business. So today he was busying himself lightly watering all the spirits behind the bar.

The light streaming in the doorway suddenly started to blink and warp, and the figure of a horseman stood inside the threshold. He removed his gloves and hat, and in doing so appeared queerly animated, his every movement causing sharply cast fluttery shadows to flicker across the room. He stepped all the way inside and stood for a moment, adjusting to the dim light. The barkeep, recognizing him immediately, greeted him with great deference and dusted off a stool for him to sit on. He said in Spanish:

'I cannot tarry long here, I must be going soon,' then he looked around the room and asked: 'Are we alone?'

The barman pointed his thumb over his right shoulder and tilted his head toward the figure in the far corner; 'Just this fat English sailor, who has been resting in that spot since they arrived, it seems.'

The horseman continued in a low Spanish voice: 'I am looking for the English captain, has he been here today?'

'He has never been here. None of the English have come here except this one,' he poked his thumb over his shoulder again, 'and one other that was brought here by Luis Loco.'

'I know the one. They passed through my *rancho* last week on their way north. When he learned I could read English he showed to me, and in the end gave to me, a number of political screeds in his possession, but they were rather poorly written things, each one disagreeing with the other in any number of particulars; he and Luis left before I could find out where he obtained the papers.'

'I didn't see those, 'smiled the bartender, 'but did he show you his money?'

The horseman shook his head.

'Take a look at this,' the barman opened a box on the shelf behind the bar and took out the note, winked, and laid the paper on the bar.

The horseman slowly picked up the bill and looked at it carefully: 'If the amount were not so high it might be taken for genuine in its general appearance,' turning it over, 'and I must say that even I have never heard before of a draught for such a kingly sum; an audacious forgery to be sure.'

He set the bill down and walked to the far side of the bar, motioning for the barman to follow him. Leaning across the bar close to him he said:

'Hector, these English are trouble. I will tell you, confidentially, that when I find this Captain Aubrey of theirs, he will be called to account for his transgressions against me, of which I can speak no more than to say he affronted my honour.'

'I am most distressed to hear of it, Sir. A very serious matter indeed, it sounds. Can I help you in any way?"

'Thank you, no. I must of course handle this myself. You may have no fear, I shall receive satisfaction, I assure you, my friend.'

'You may find him ashore if you ask after him at the embarcadero, that is all I can tell you.'

'Perhaps that is what I shall do then,' he put his gloves and hat back on, 'Good day to you, Hector.'

'Good luck, Don Onofre, go with God,' said the barman, returning to watering the spirits, but distracted as he now was, several minutes passed before he noticed that the fat *Ingles marinaros* was gone, and with him, the note.

Following Captain Aubrey's orders to the last letter as he always did, Bonden had been working since morning directing the watering, redoubling those efforts in fact, but doing so in such a way so as to not attract undue attention to it. Both starboard and larboard watches had orders to report by two bells in the second dog watch, as they would be needed for 'ships' duties' in the morning, Bonden's vague concoction, but true as far as it went. Nic Crofter and Tanzi volunteered to fetch the men at the mission and had already returned with everyone except Fat-Arse Jenks, whom an angry Father De La Valle said had been missing for three days, and had apparently taken the mission's best mule along with a fine saddle. Bonden knew that if they didn't find him before they weighed he would surely be listed as a deserter, so he sent his friend, Awkward Davis, after him with strict orders to return by two bells himself, no matter what.

For Bonden, his duties were clear; for Stephen and Jack, however, it was not at all clear what they should next do. Jack wished fervently that he could stay aboard until they weighed. Wished, in fact, that he had never gone ashore in the first instance, where so often his fortunes were reversed it seemed. For Stephen's part, he had spent the better portion of the night staring at the draught with a degree still of misbelief, and mulling every detail in his mind, all the while praying for a blessed *deus ex machina* to extract him from the most dangerously exposed situation ever he had found himself in during his long career in intelligence work.

First thing in the morning Stephen had met with Luis Loco at the embarcadero and inquired regarding the 'pretty paper' that the dog had stolen the night before at the hide house; where had he gotten it? Did he have others or know of any others? But Luis had no answers, only his own questions; Did Stephen know what the dog had done with it? Why should he tell him the whereabouts of the others? Was Stephen trying to steal his pretty papers? And so forth, growing increasingly belligerent. Stephen attempted to very gently turn the conversation around, indicating that perhaps if he were shown the papers, he should like to trade for them. This comment provoked ambivalence in his demeanor, vacillating between his shrewful, covetous trepidation, and his beady-eyed, grasping avarice. After some inquiries regarding specifically what Stephen had for trade, his suspicion overpowered his greed, and he ran off abruptly in mid sentence, leapt on his horse, and rode off into the hills to the north.

Stephen had asked Lale if he would go after Luis Loco, and now, in the early afternoon, Stephen and Kieki Hae waited together on the embarcadero, the little shepherd dog curled up in the coolness of Stephen's shadow. She lifted her head and looked to the north, and Lale appeared over the hilltop.

'Aroha aikáne,' Lalli flashed his huge teeth, 'Tepano, what are you doing sitting here in the sun? Hop on back and I'll take you to

the hide house for supper.'

'I was waiting for Luis Loco, you did not find him I take it?'

'Of course I did, Tepano, I found him right away, in the hills along the coast just north of here, on the very high cliffs over the ocean where the Indians often like to hunt. I told him you wished to meet with him again, and I watched as he turned around and rode in this direction. Then I turned eastward to a place I know, a place one of the Indians showed me once, where these grow,' Lale reached into a bag and tossed Stephen a China orange, 'and I didn't see him again after that.'

'Lale, just where is this hunting ground?'

'It is very high on a sheer cliff, on a medium-sized jutland that pokes out about two miles north of the beach where Captain Jack went swimming with us.'

Stephen turned around and there was Jack himself, just arriving in Jack Ditler's boat at the embarcadero. Jack had spent the morning hours taking care of the very ugly matter of the two prisoners' bodies. Martin had again presided over a respectful memorial service in the *Hermiones'* brig that seemed to satisfy everyone, and that situation appeared quelled, at least for now. Of course this matter of Stephen and himself retrieving these confidential papers was a far more daunting basket of snakes.

'You're just in time, Jack,' Stephen turned to Lale: 'Pray, could you accompany us to the area where you last saw Luis?'

'I'll bring Kiristopa along to help us; he's got sharp young eyes.'

'You are very good, Lale, Thank you.'

'*Aroha* Captain Jack, I still have your horse, tied over to the hide house. If I take you and Tepano the long way, perhaps we may race again today? You were very good sport in our last joust!'

'My very best compliments, Lale, and thank you,' Jack started toward the hide houses, 'Indeed, that was a capital ride the other day, but today we've no time for horseplay, there's not a moment to lose.'

Lale said to Jack Ditler:

'We'll be going up to the Indian hunting cliffs,' he pointed north along the water's edge, 'You know the place?'

Ditler nodded, 'I'll be here until about mid-tide, going out, I'd say,' he walked backward toward his ferry and waved, 'maybe I'll see you before then, but if not, just go ahead and use the dory.'

Lale arranged for the hostelry, although this time they all rode without saddles, while the Sandwich Islanders dispenced with even the blankets Jack and Stephen used. Lale fashioned war bridles from the long lariats around the horses' necks, and in the event the arrangement answered perfectly for the small bridal path, or *camino de herraduro*, which would take them up to the high coastal ledges. They would not need the bulky *tapaderos* to protect their feet from so much barbed vegetation, as the moister coastal air promoted a bit more greenery and a bit less cactus and thistles, although both Kieki Hae and Náenáe attached themselves to innumerable foxtails along the way, and Kiristopa had to stop once and dig two little mace-like burrs, which Lale called 'goatheads,' out of one of the horses hooves.

Stephen was bringing up the rear of their party, and Jack fell back in line to ride abreast of him. He turned to Jack and, speaking very softly, said:

'I now have good reason to believe this Luis Loco chap has at least some of the rest of the notes, and may know where to start looking for any others. Jack, I am still incredulous about this entire affair. I cannot imagine--and I have spent the day and night turning it over--I cannot imagine how this witling came into possession of these papers.'

Jack looked down at Stephen, who was mounted on a small bay mare, and then ahead to where the Sandwich Islanders rode, just out of earshot.

'Stephen, I think I've smoked at least part of this mess, although the larger portion of it still eludes me as well.'

Stephen looked at Jack and blinked his eyes.

'I believe I know the name of the thief who took the...the confidential papers in the first place...'

Stephen blinked again, 'You amaze me brother.'

'Well, I still don't know how he took it, or certainly how he found it, or even how he knew it was there to be found. But more to the point, I don't know any more than you about the current whereabouts of the ...documents.'

'Pray, what did you discover?'

'You recall the mutineer, David Jonas, who was shot and lost overboard, do you not? Well, it may have been a very clever ruse in a plot to escape, which, God help me, it appears this hedge-creeper has done, and into New Spain here, with the entire contents of that damnedable box.'

'I must say, Jack, you have a flair for intelligence.'

'I certainly don't have the stomach for it, I can tell you that, nor any flair either, I'm afraid. I was merely aboard *Enderby* on account of the two other mutineers that had capped it, and Tanzi and Nic button-hooked me over to the starboard chains and showed me the evidence they'd found; it was young Nic Crofter who smoked it, really, not I, Stephen. Jonas wasn't lost overboard, he was a stowaway, or one might say a "towaway," clapped on to the end of a long line trailing behind *Enderby*. Then I remembered that a couple of days before we made port here I went to my cabin and one of the stern windows was open all the way, something Killick or I would never do. And then there was the matter of the sailor that arrived here ahead of us, remember?'

Of course, thought Stephen, how could he have failed to penetrate that?

'They said Luis Loco was last seen with somebody from the ship, and yet we were the first ashore, or so we thought. Jack Ditler hadn't taken him or anyone else ashore, but I have to presume he's an excellent swimmer. So if Luis Loco doesn't have all the rest of the papers, he shall have to lead us to this lurcher Jonas.'

'Getting any information from Luis could prove very difficult.

He's a naturally intransigent cove, and, as Lalli says, it's not for nothing he is called "loco." He's most mercurial; I might say undevinable. But who else knows any of this?'

'Just Tanzi and Nic, and I've given them a direct order never to speak of it to anyone.

'Stephen, I will tell you that my primary interest is in recovering the papers, not Jonas. I wish to ship as soon as possible.'

They came to the crest of a low coastal hill where there stood an old and rather tall oak, at least it towered above the few other, younger, scrub oaks around it. They secured the horses to it, and Lale said:

'Do you recognize this tree, Captain Jack? She is your friend, I think.'

Jack looked at Lale with a puzzled expression, thinking for a moment. Lale pointed due north along the shoreline.

'There is the beach where we bathed, and this is the marker tree that shows at what depth the waves shall break, do you see?'

'Well, right you are, Lale,' Jack looked along the curving coastline, and from this distance the waves appeared as three or four very thin, white jagged lines of spilt flour, constantly forming, and then disappearing parallel to the shore, as they were swept into it. 'I make it about two miles from here to our beach; can you see it, Stephen?'

They divided into three groups: Jack would walk south along the coastal mesa to the high coastal cliffs, Stephen and Kieki Hae would traverse the north coast along the low hilltops and then circle back south, and Lale, Kiristopa, and Náenáe would walk east for a distance and circle back southwesterly toward Jack's position, where everyone would regroup and return to the horses, or perhaps continue the search elsewhere nearby.

Jack made his way at a measured rate, observing his footing with each step on the uneven bluffs, and also pausing with each step, looking hard in the distances all about for any sign of Luis Loco. Some time passed before he reached the very highest cliffs, perched precipitously overhanging the churning ocean, which, at this tide, was some twenty fathoms below. Jack looked up ahead about fifty yards and there was Luis, standing in the Indian footpath that ran along the cliff's edge. Jack cried out to him, he turned and plainly saw Jack, who smiled and asked in his best Spanish to speak him a moment.

Luis looked frightened by seeing Jack, but he stepped quite close to the edge and looked down at the water very closely for a moment. He then moved several large steps back, looked at Jack who was racing to get to him, looked back at the cliff, took a swift running start, and, to Jack's astonished eyes, leapt off the bluff's edge with a fierce abandon.

Jack, who had been running toward him, insensibly slowed his pace with each advancing step until finally he was just standing there, mouth open, staring at the spot from where Luis had disappeared. At some length, his composure restored, Jack slowly shuffled his way closer to the edge of the bluff, but the terrain took a slight, steep, downhill dip right at the edge, and the sandy soil seemed of dubious stability under Jack's fifteen stone tread. When he was six feet from the drop off he got down on his hands and knees and very charily inched forward. At this angle it was difficult to know just how many steps one could take before the *terra* became too impossibly precipitous to be *firma*, and Jack wasn't sure he could safely get a look directly straight down without actually falling. However, Luis had apparently had no trouble from a standing position, so despite his serious trepidation about the way this soil felt under him, and the way it made him feel to look up at the vast seascape below him, he inched ahead until he could just get his eyes over the edge, the rest of Jack's body was splayed out to the four points of the compass and clapped onto Mother Earth for dear life. When he looked down, however, the view was blocked by grasses that sprouted along the top six to ten feet of the bluff. Jack slowly began to move ever so slowly, to go just a bit further over the edge, when suddenly he was startled by a duck which stuck her neck out from her cubby in the cliff-face and quacked loudly, right in Jack's face.

'I shall attribute my next grey hair to you,' Jack muttered as she hid back in her nest below a thatch of grass and wildflowers.

Ever more warily Jack crept out to the very rim, and could now finally look straight down. When he did the view made his breath catch and his bowels clench like a fist. Jack had gambolled about many a tall ships' masthead since he was a mere boy, to be sure, but this was different; there would be nothing to grab onto in a fall, and, of course, it was many times higher than the tallest ship-of-the-line.

Far down below, the great ocean surged against the foot of the cliff and then retreated, exposing a five or six foot wide, rock-strewn beach. Luis Loco's body was not visible, but the surf could answer for that. To the right of Jack were two rather large rocks that poked out of the water and in their direct vicinity were several large boils, telling of more of the same submerged nearby. To Jack's left he could see the cliff curving around to the west, gradually lowering to the sea about a half of a mile or so away. Jack could also make out what appeared to be several sea caves in the wall of the cliffs to his left, with countless sea birds perched in the pock-marked rock face above them.

Something moving caught Jack's attention and he racked his eyes back to the mouth of the furthest cave. There was a man going into the cave, walking in waist deep water, and then pulling his way on to the rocks and out of sight. It was Luis Loco to be sure, and by his movements he was none the worse for the wear from a fall that seemed to promise certain death. Jack lay there watching for a spell until he was sure Luis would not soon come back into view. He took one more look straight down, and again felt his innards clutch at the thought of falling from this lofty place.

Jack crawled slowly backward away from the edge a distance and heard a horse coming as he got to his feet and turned around.

'Defend yourself, sir, I demand satisfaction of you!' Don Onofre's horse was still at a gallop as he stepped off with two sharpened foils in the glove of his right hand, and then threw one of them to Jack.

Catching it, Jack took a quick glance over his shoulder and stepped further from the edge.

'Don Onofre, there is a misunderstanding. I do not wish to duel with you, sir. I bid you no ill-will at all.'

'No misunderstanding,' and he thrust his blade and stabbed Jack straight through his left arm, 'It is I who wishes the duel, and you know perfectly well why, sir.'

The pierce of Don Onofre's sword was blindingly painful, and the blade's retraction was twice again as stinging, enough that it crossed Jack's mind that he mustn't faint just now, not in this predicament, with the cliff just a few downhill steps astern of him. He wildly swung his sword back and forth in front of him a few times, like a batsman taking practise in cricket, as he tried to get further from the edge, but Don Onofre deftly withdrew and Jack just whipped at the air with a high-pitched whooshing sound, reinforcing what Jack had already been thinking; that this was a fight he didn't belong in. He had never before used a foil in his life, usually fighting with a saber in his right hand, a dirk in his left, and a pistol in his breeches belt. Were he so armed now, even with his back to the sea as it is, three such men as Don Onofre would be no real match for Jack, but with this foil he was useless.

'Don Onofre,' Jack held his weapon at guard, 'I must warn you, sir, do not act so rashly, and pray, do *not* stick me again with that darning needle of yours. Surely we can conduct ourselves as gentlemen.'

Don Onofre thrust again, and this time Jack instinctively blocked it, using his foil like a cutlass, and the resulting strike was only a glancing nick to Jack's left thigh.

'Damn your eyes, man!' Jack charged at him swinging his foil, but expecting to try to thrust with it properly when he could create an opportunity. He had been caught completely off-guard, and now, he thought, he must try to unbalance Don Onofre as well. But where the first strike to Jack's arm had somehow avoided severing any large arteries, the second happened to find a small vessel just above the knee, and bursts of blood squirted between Jack's fingers as he held it with his left hand. Between the two wounds the clothing on his left side was now wonderfully horribly bloody, and the odd thought flitted through Jack's mind that Killick would be extremely upset with him.

Jack had triumphed in many far less civil battles before this, but just as Stephen had found Las Pulgas an implausibly skilled English billiards player, Jack was now discovering the Don to be a peerless duelist with the French foil, very likely the finest swordsman Jack had ever seen. Jack made a clumsy poke that forced Don Onofre to take a single defensive step back, and Jack took one more step away from the edge to get side-by-side with him. But before Jack could properly shift his weight off his back foot Don Onofre took another withering thrust, and this time with a keen deceptive skill, holding his body in such a way, and parrying at just the correct angle, such that his sword was rendered almost invisible to Jack. All Jack could see was Las Pulgas' hand shield, and so he put his right arm straight away from him and concentrated on striking the handle of Don Onofre's foil.

Their handshields clashed together very hard, and as they pushed away from each other Jack noted that he had the advantage of Don Onofre in reach. Despite his loss of blood, Jack was still clearly the far stronger of the two men, and, quickly formulating a strategy, Jack thought he might risk one more wound to get inside of Don Onofre's sword, that is, too close for him to use his foil end effectively, and perhaps, Jack thought, Las Pulgas could be disarmed and wrestled to the ground, putting an end to this nonsense. He held his foil at full length straight out from his body, waiting for the next strike and watching only Las Pulgas' handshield, as the Don bobbed about in graceful, well-practised motions.

Don Onofre's blade took another lethal pass at Jack, aimed to pierce his heart this time, and Jack responded by taking one step to his right while swinging his sword right at the incoming hand guard. Their blades slid against each other with a grating sound until their hands again collided, this time with a great banging thud. Jack bent his elbow and stepped close to Las Pulgas, then with a brisk motion he pulled his foil back and with the handle of the sword struck Las Pulgas on his forehead, opening a gash in it.

This enraged Las Pulgas who stepped back and whipped Jack across the face with the side of his foil. Don Onofre was seething now, but still in complete control, and still displaying superior fencing form. Jack had paid rather dearly for his momentary advance, the Don's harsh rebuke had his cheek and ear burning terribly, but at least, thought Jack, it appears I have a chance of simply defending myself, but for how long?

With Las Pulgas next stroke he would find out. Again Jack watched the hand shield approach, again he held his foil out to meet it, but this time as the two blades began to mesh Don Onofre lifted his wrist ever so slightly and spun the tip in a clock-wise motion. There was the sound of metal against metal as they slid together, and then a high, silvery ringing sound as Jack's sword flew from his hand and went tumbling through the air to land on the ground several feet to Jack's left.

Don Onofre came out of his fencers' crouch and slowly stood straight to attention, holding his foil blade upright, directly between his eyes.

'Prepare to die where you stand, sir!' Las Pulgas lifted his his right knee to deliver the *coup de gras*.

Suddenly there were hoof beats coming from behind them and a loud shout of:

'No! No! Not my Captain Aubrey!' as Fat-Arse Jenks appeared over the crest astride a very large mule that was charging at full speed toward Las Pulgas. When the mule saw the edge she placed all four hooves forward and bucked Jenks right over her head. He tried to land on Don Onofre, but instead found the Don's blade, which ran him clear through his chest, and Las Pulgas watched as Jenks fell over the bluff, still impaled on the foil. When Las Pulgas turned back, Jack was holding the one remaining foil against his neck.

'Let's don't any more of us die here today,' said Jack, 'shall we agree? I beg you, sir, this matter has gone too far already.'

Las Pulgas nodded agreement and Jack withdrew the foil from his throat and threw it off the side; it made a faint whistling sound as it fell. But Don Onofre was a man unaccustomed to the gracious acceptance of defeat, and as he stood up he pulled a small dagger from his boot and came straight for Jack, still determined to receive satisfaction. Jack feinted to his right and then fell forward to his left on top of Las Pulgas' charging feet. The Don went to the ground face first, dropping the knife which landed very close to the cliff. He crawled over and reached for it, and when he turned around his right foot slipped off the grassy edge.

'Oh...' said Don Onofre, looking down at his feet and trying to catch his balance, 'oh, no.'

He tried to pull his right leg back up, but instead the ground crumbled under his other foot and it slipped off as well, leaving him dangling, his fists scrambling at the slippery sandstone, while he still held to the dagger. His eyes grew very wide with terror, and he hissed:

'Madre de Dios!' before silently plummetting, helpless, to the sea far, far below.

'Aué! Ho'okahe koko!' shouted Kiristopa, 'Captain Jack, what has happened to you?'

Jack had been sitting on the ground, holding his wounds and still trying to stem the bleeding in his leg when the Sandwich Islanders arrived. Náenáe ran over to Jack and touched his cheek with her nose, then licked him twice where Las Pulgas blade had flogged him.

'Thank you, Náenáe, that felt rather nice,' he twisted around to look at Lale and Kiristopa, 'There's been an accident, Don Onofre is dead; he fell from the cliff here. His horse has run off.'

'And the buffalo man, the man that was on the mule?' Lale gathered up the reins of the lathered beast and secured the ends under a heavy rock.

'The same.'

'Kiristopa and I saw the Don ride by us at some distance. Then, when we saw the buffalo man following him as fast as ever a mule could run, we decided to follow them both. But what has happened to you, Captain Jack?'

'Well, Lale, I shant play fiddle for a few days, it appears.'

Kiristopa pointed to the markings in the dirt where Las Pulgas had slipped over, '*Há úle laua?* Both fell?'

Jack nodded.

'*Aroha ino!* What a pity!' Kiristopa looked at Jack and Lale, 'You know, one can leap from this spot and live, if you know how.'

'I hope you haven't tried that,' scolded Lale, 'especially not at this tide.'

'I just witnessed Luis Loco do it not half an hour ago,' said Jack.

'That fits,' said Lale, without intending the remark's sardonic drollery.

'Both of their bodies are still down there,' said Kiristopa, who was now perilously close himself, looking down.

'Lale, could we get the horses down there? I need to retrieve Jenks' body.'

'We can get the horses, and the mule too, down to the shore, the path is just two cable's lengths to the south or so from here. And there is a natural sort of fresh water well there also, if it has water right now.'

The islanders headed off to get the horses, Kiristopa still muttering: *'Aroha ino,'* and similar sounding, sing-songy lamentations in the Sandwich Islanders musical tongue, while Náenáe remained behind, keeping close at Jack's side, where they waited together. In course, the islanders returned on horseback with Jack's horse in tow, and they had found Stephen and Kieki Hae as well. Lale had also brought a brace of long, sturdy-looking cane stalks he had cut.

'Ah, Doctor, you are here! It is so very good to see you, and it appears I may be in need of your services. Have you any stitching thread?'

'Moses in the mountains, Jack! They told me you had been cut somehow, but this?' Stephen got down off of his horse for a closer look.

'I have this,' Stephen took his cravat off and tied it around Jack's leg with his handkerchief pressed over the wound. Turning his attention to Jack's arm he said:

'This one looks like you were punctured, Jack.'

'Indeed, I was pierced through by Don Onofre's sword.'

Stephen looked quizzically at his friend.

'Well, Stephen, I'm afraid I was brought up upon a lee shore by Doña-Fior during our visit. I had hoped nothing like this would come of it, but...'

Of course, thought Stephen, this would explain Jack's preoccupation with leaving as soon as possible, despite the probable escapee on the loose.

'What do you intend to do about him?' Stephen pointed his nose in the direction of the spot where Don Onofre had fallen.

'Right now I want to get Jenk's body out of there, and back to the ship for a proper sea burial tomorrow; Stephen, the man surely saved my life up here today. But I wish to continue our pursuit of Luis Loco as well--we're very close, I believe--and it looks like we can do both at once,' Jack winced as Stephen knotted the dressing over his arm wounds, 'the fact is, it really was an accident with the Don; I didn't push him off--he slipped off the edge,' Jack grimaced again as he tried to pull himself aboard his horse without using his left arm, and Lale leaned from his horse, reached under Jack's shoulder, and hoisted him up on the horse's back.

When they reached the cliff bottom it was not far from the cave Jack had seen Luis Loco enter; it was a very large-mouthed, high-ceilinged, somewhat horseshoe-shaped, sea cavern of a sort, with two openings to the sea and a third, large skylight opening to the inland side that let in some sunlight. Stephen stayed with the horses, and Jack and the islanders carefully made their way in the water across the mouth of the first cave and along the rock-strewn shore toward the bodies. The tide had been on the ebb, and they were able to alternately paddle or wade their way along, sometimes swimming out a short distance to avoid getting caught between the rocks and incoming breakers. Jenks and Las Pulgas still lay side by side in the sand, their faces and limbs now disfigured into mishappen shapes by the impact of the terrible fall. Las Pulgas' foil was still embedded in Jenks, and Jack found the blade end of the other foil sticking out of the sand a few feet away. He put both in his breeches belt, and the three men began the labourious process of getting Jenk's body back to the horses and shore. Jack turned to Lale and asked:

'Do you think Jack Ditler's dory could float Fat-Ar...er, rather, Jenks' body with one of us to discreetly pull him over to *Surprise*?'

'I will do it, Captain Jack,' said Lale, 'and which I will pull you and Tepano over first, and then return for the body.'

'Thank you very much, Lale. Now, Lale, you understand that the Don and I had a misunderstanding, and there was no need for a duel, do you not? I hope I can rely on both you and Kiristopa to keep this business a secret between us. When they find his body, no one needs know the exact circumstances of the Don's death, just that it was an accident; after all, this could needlessly dishonour his memory, or cause harm to his widow's reputation, do we understand each other?'

Lale smiled and nodded, looking at Kiristopa who agreed, adding:

'You and Doctor Tepano are *aikáne* to *kanakas*, Captain Jack, Don Onofre never was.'

By the time they brought Jenks' body ashore Stephen had watered the horses and had been waiting for them. Lale immediately set to the task of constructing a very robust *travaille* from the stout cane he had cut, and then attached it to Jenks' mule, but Jack had him remove it, saying:

'Before we go back I wish to try and find Luis Loco once more.'

Pulling a leather pocket book from his coat, Jack approached Stephen and, opening it, said quietly:

'I found another one of those blasted notes in Jenks' coat, and I found this in the Don's breast pocket,' Jack handed Stephen the note with some other sheaths.

Stephen gingerly looked at one corner of the parchment documents and sighed, looking skyward.

'Thank the dear!' It appeared all three cover letters would be fully intact once properly dried out. 'And thank you, Jack, for finding these. This is some small relief, at least.'

The two Sandwich Islanders now approached Jack and Stephen, Kiristopa somewhat diffident, Lale directly behind him, hand on his shoulder:

'Go on, Kiristopa,' and, with a nod of encouragement, 'tell them...'

Jack and Stephen looked blankly at the normally chatty island boy, whose tongue now seemed tethered, until he finally said:

'Captain Jack, Tepano, you really look for Luis Loco? This was not Lale's joke?'

Jack continued looking at him while Stephen blinked behind his blue spectacles.

'I know about a secret place Luis Loco goes. I followed him once,' he looked at Jack, 'That day I, too, saw him take that dead man's leap and live.' He looked down at the beach and accessed the height of the tide, 'We will need maybe couple small torches, I can show you.'

'How far is it?' asked Stephen, and Kiristopa pointed off to his left at the cave mouth.

'You can see it. We're there right now.'

Lale got two small torches going and Kiristopa and Stephen kept them dry walking across the mouth of the cave along the tops of the now mostly exposed rocks. Kieki Hae didn't wish to swim, so she stayed on shore, pacing nervously between Lale and Náenáe, stopping occasionally to anxiously watch Stephen and utter little suppressed yelps.

'This is the place, Tepano,' Kiristopa put his hand against the solid rock wall of the cave mouth.

'Is Kiristopa joking now?' asked Stephen, taking off his spectacles.

'No, no. Right here!' Kiristopa put his hands on either side of a vertical crack in the rock face that ran about twelve feet high and perhaps only nine inches wide and said:

'This. This is a place, inside here.'

With that he turned his body sideways and stepped into the crack, holding the torch in his left hand while motioning to Stephen to follow him with his right.

Immediately past the opening Stephen discovered the crack widened away from itself into a tiny ante chamber that had a solid rock wall to it, beaten smooth as whale skin by time and tide. Kiristopa pointed down and held out his torch:

'Look there, do you see this white rock? We must step over it and then get down on all fours, understand?'

Stephen nodded.

'For a bit, even with the torch, you won't be able to see much. Careful not to burn yourself.'

The white rock was quite smooth and slippery, and one had to straddle it with care to avoid falling or dropping the torch. Once over it, Kiristopa crouched down and all but disappeared in blackness. Stephen bent down, and there, incredibly, was a worm-hole opening about twenty inches in diameter, with Kiristopa's legs and feet disappearing into it. Stephen crawled about eight feet along this way until he felt the ground become wet beach sand beneath him, and emerged from the worm-hole only to find he now had to squeeze out from under a large flat rock.

'I'm in!' he heard Kiristopa say just up ahead, and, sticking his face and his torch down where Stephen could see him he said:

'You are almost there, Tepano.'

At last the rock above Steven angled away, giving him some

headroom, and then suddenly there he was, standing in a chamber deep within the cliffs above, Kiristopa nervously giggling like a monkey.

'Don't be scared in here, Tepano,' Kiristopa giggled again, and in the torchlight Stephen could see his breath, as on a winter day, 'I get scared enough for two of us. But look:' he held his torch up and walked backward for Stephen to view the cave.

It was shaped like a narrow slice of pie, a good thirty feet deep, the worm-hole entry being at the point of the pie slice, where the ceiling was about four feet, but as it vaunted back in the chamber it rose to about twelve feet.

'Be careful not to trip,' said Kiristopa pointing to a small, sharp rock sticking out of the sandy ground, 'and here is the table.'

At the back of the cave there was indeed a flat square rock that seemed to be naturally hewn furniture, just the correct height, location, and size for gaming or dining, and symmetrically placed there by some fussy domestic steward of the sea.

Kiristopa held his torch toward the back wall, 'There are the shelves, you see?'

Above the table rock, high up the cave wall, above the tide mark, were natural cubbies protruding from the rock face. Stephen climbed on the table and easily stepped up the rocky wall to the highest shelf. He held his torch up for a closer look and saw something pushed into the back corner. He reached in and pulled out a folded patch of tarpaulin, quite filthy, with a bit of string tied about it. The air in this highest part of the cave was unbearably thick with moisture and Stephen's breath was now in billowing clouds around him. He took it down and opened the horrible thing on the table. There was a momentary clearing in the weather as Stephen breathlessly counted, and then counted once again, to be certain. All ten of the remaining missing notes were there.

A small block was rigged to a spar and hung off the deck like a davit to bring Jenks' body aboard *Surprise*, but it still took some help from Lale for Awkward Davis--the strongest man on either ship--to sadly hoist his friend's great heft all the way up from the dory. Jack stood on the quarterdeck with Stephen, Kiristopa, and the dogs, and watched as eight seamen carried the body back to the orlop, and Jack vowed:

'I shall have church rigged at sea tomorrow and give him the service that befits his heroism today.'

'The *kanakas* all wish you would stay some more,' said Lale with a sheepish smile, 'maybe until Captain Jack can play fiddle again?'

'Well, I wish for that too, Lale. Another carefree day at the beach would be capital, but I'm afraid my presence here could no longer be carefree--and it never really was in the first instance. No, it just won't do to have a post captain scampering about like a merry Andrew, smoking rumbowlin and consorting with...well, it just won't do, that's all.

'But I want you to have this, Lale.'

Jack took out a small pouch of superfine Pomeranian sludge, 'This should clear your scrutineers loupe admirably, and this,' Jack reached into the other side of his coat and produced a telescope that had been the *Enderby's* number two night glass, 'may help you teach the squeakers more of your marvelous navigation.'

Stephen then pressed upon Lale a copy of his *Suggestions for the Amelioration of Sick Bays*, 'It's the only of my books I have with me...' along with the sheet music for the Crouperin, 'In the hope we can play it together again some day.'

Lale looked at the gifts in his hands, his face frozen in a stolid expression, save for the moisture in his eyes.

'From all my many English words, where can I find those that I need now, my *aikánes?*

'Someday, perhaps, I shall look through this fine glass and see you returning, and when I do we shall play this Crouperin again, and have a fine good time of it! *Aroha*, Tepano, and *aroha*, Captain Jack.'

He slung the glass over his shoulder and, holding the book and Náenáe in one arm, climbed over the side and down the chains to the dory. Stephen and Jack stood silently, watching the dory pull away, Náenáe standing at the stern looking back toward *Surprise*. She barked twice and Kieki Hae made a high-pitched whine and paced back and forth along Jack's usual path across the quarterdeck.

'Well my little friend, what will it be?' said Stephen, and she whined twice more, and then ran and leapt atop the taffrail, and perched there, looking first at Lale and then back at Stephen. Náenáe barked again and Kieki Hae looked out at the dory, letting out a cry while she screwed up her courage. With one last adoring look at Stephen, she barked a good-bye and dove off the rail into the waters of San Diego Bay to follow Lale and Náenáe home.

Stephen and Jack stood in silence watching at the stern as Lale slowed to let Kieki Hae catch up, and pulled her into the dory; and they continued watching for a long time, staring into the spot where they had disappeared into the black night. Then Jack finally turned and said:

'You understand, of course, Stephen, that for everyone's sake I shall have to omit from the ships' official log any mention whatsoever of our time here. With any luck, this story will never have to be told.'

By this time tomorrow, if the breeze held, *Surprise* would be well along on her way south again, and San Diego far astern of her forever.